Gavin and Greneknighte

GAVIN

AND

GRENEKNIGHTE

a present-day reimagining of
Sir Gawain and the Green Knight

Philip Sealey

Matador
9 Priory Business Park,
Wistow Road, Kibworth Beauchamp,
Leicestershire. LE8 0RX
Tel: 0116 279 2299
Email: books@troubador.co.uk
Web: www.troubador.co.uk/matador
Twitter: @matadorbooks

ISBN 978 1789015 560

British Library Cataloguing in Publication Data.
A catalogue record for this book is available from the British Library.

Printed and bound by CPI Group (UK) Ltd, Croydon, CR0 4YY
Typeset in 11pt Adobe Garamond Pro by Troubador Publishing Ltd, Leicester, UK

Matador is an imprint of Troubador Publishing Ltd

If ye wyl lysten this laye bot on litel quile,
I schal telle hit as-tit, as I in toun herde,
 with tonge,
  As hit is stad and stoken
  In stori stif and stronge
  With lel letteres loken,
  In londe so hatz ben longe.
                            – *Sir Gawayn and ye Grene Knyght,* Anonymous

He broke off. Flames glided on the river, small green flames, red flames, white flames, pursuing, overtaking, joining, crossing each other – then separating slowly or hastily. The traffic of the great city went on in the deepening night upon the sleepless river. We looked on, waiting patiently – there was nothing else to do till the end of the flood; but it was only after a long silence… that we knew we were fated, before the ebb began to run, to hear about one of Marlow's inconclusive experiences.

                            – *Heart of Darkness*, Joseph Conrad

O you who turn the wheel and look to windward,
Consider Phlebas, who was once handsome and tall as you.
— *The Waste Land IV: Death by Water,* T. S. Eliot

If a man could pass through Paradise in a dream, and have
a flower presented to him as a pledge that his soul had really
been there, and if he found that flower in his hand when he
awake — Aye, what then?

— *Anima Poetae,* Samuel Taylor Coleridge

The Challenge

The *Astarte*, our pleasure steamer for the last night of the year, rocked at anchor by Swan Lane Pier. A few hundred yards downstream, London Bridge boomed and vibrated in the fading light with the noise of its traffic, and on either side, early revellers were flowing along the embankment paths towards the pubs and restaurants that lined the riverside. Like an ice-blue stalagmite, a monstrous nail bolted to the City's floor, as though it would scratch the face of God, the Shard rose up beside us into the murk. It was the city's truest emblem, I had come to believe: cold and heartless and spitefully beautiful.

I had arrived early, wanting to search out a seat in the dining room safe from the draughts that afflicted such cruises down the river to Greenwich and sometimes beyond, and which I hoped would enable me to keep away from those I had no wish to spend an evening with; listening to talk about deals done on smartphones and tablets, which would become the stuff of unborn bankers' dreams, was not my idea of an enjoyable way to pass the time on the last night of the year, or any night for that matter.

Phelbas, our Phoenician Sailor, as he liked to style himself, insisting as he did so on the curious spelling which placed the 'e' before the 'l' – and not as the name appeared in 'that poem you might have read', as he put it – had greeted me as I stepped off the gangplank. After all, these annual excursions of ours, with his dark figure at the wheel, had been taking place on this same evening for as long as I could remember, and it was I, your Narrator, who made the arrangements, visited him and Elyssa, his wife, on their barge moored upriver from Battersea Bridge, opposite the old Lots Road power station, and then pressured my colleagues, the younger ones especially, with talk of team spirit and camaraderie, and of how something memorable, even if it was only another of Henley's unlikely stories, was bound to occur; which, if they failed to attend, they would forever regret having missed.

The evening had become, as you can see, something of a ritual.

Phelbas and I exchanged a few words, while Elyssa, the only woman who would be present during the evening, with a smile of recognition took my coat and disappeared. And that was one of the rules: that there would be no wives or partners (no 'underdressed girlfriends', a Director had once stipulated to me) to distract the male employees on this occasion. Though I found the proscription ridiculous – as if the Bank was a male-only club of some kind – I was prepared to go along with it for this one night of the year, as something in me liked to preserve the Bank's old customs, the faint glimpses of its origins that could be seen in some of the paintings that lined the corridors. The past, to me, was worth respecting, a reminder of the way things once had been, not something to be swept away in the name of a progress whose benefits sometimes seemed questionable.

Of course, there were many who found the idea completely unreasonable: the juniors would much prefer to be with their friends in some rowdy pub, and the female staff rolled their eyes at me in disbelief when I asserted that this was the Bank's tradition.

'You mean, *your* tradition!' Helena, one of the senior accountants, had said to me crossly, before telling me that this year the women would be having their own New Year's Eve celebration; but I took it in good part, even if what she said about it being my tradition wasn't true. I had been at the Bank, running what used to be the personnel department but was now something called human resources, longer than them and knew about these things. Only a few of the Directors and Henley had more years of service.

Phelbas asked, in his accented English, how the markets were doing in these difficult times (after all, trading ran in his Levantine blood), and about my two sons. He knew my wife and I had long since lived apart and I suspect he found this difficult to understand, but I had grown familiar with my own company and the small house I had bought in one of the less gentrified streets of Whitechapel suited me well enough. I had once imagined a different future for myself – some kind of shining career as a literary critic, with a position as editor of a respected, subscription-only journal as a sideline – but after my inability to live up to my parents' expectations at Oxford, the Bank had appeared like a landfall looming out of the sea-fog, and it had drawn me, like everyone else who would be present this evening, into its labyrinth. Of that earlier, half-dreamed life, all that remained were the notebooks full of incomplete reviews and essays, and a lingering resentment at my own insufficiency.

'You've seen the weather reports?' Phelbas asked once I had answered his questions.

I looked up at the overcast sky, where a full moon was scheduled to appear later, and nodded.

'Windy with heavy rain.'

He sniffed the darkness like a dog that scents a change in the weather. He scratched the silvery stubble on his cheek.

'The winds are coming from the north-east, the Russian steppes; places I've never been, where no ships sail. They will be here by the early hours of the New Year, racing up this old river into the heart of the city. We both know what that will be like.'

'Too rough for us, you mean?'

'It's a question of the boat. The *Astarte* is not built for stormy weather. She is, as you know, a pleasure steamer.'

I recalled him telling me, years before, of how he had bought the boat from an Armenian ferry owner in Istanbul, had refitted her himself, and then sailed her with a crew of the dispossessed from the Bosphorus wharves, up the Danube, past ports of legend, through half of Europe to the Rhine, and then across the North Sea to the provincial banality of the Thames. I reminded him of the story, wondering at the concern a man of such seafaring experience was showing.

'We waited for weeks in Rotterdam until the sea was as flat and grey as glass,' he answered. 'And it would be unwise to underestimate the tricks this river can play.'

'Are you saying we should spend the evening here at the moorings, without casting off at all?'

He smiled. 'No, I don't think such measures will be necessary. One has to be prepared, that's all. And if the winds arrive earlier than expected, we can always ride them out somewhere along the way.' He paused, and I saw what I took to be an ironic glitter in his eyes. 'I wanted you to be aware of the situation. Perhaps you might want to say something when our passengers start arriving.' He paused once more, and I waited, knowing he had been leading up to something. 'In the end, you are the Captain.'

I laughed, but he caught my arm with his strong fingers. 'The *Astarte*, the Lady of the Sea, is my ship, yes. I bought her, I steer her up and down this river for a living. But I only turn the wheel and look from where the wind is blowing. You, my friend, are the Captain.'

He turned away to say something to Elyssa in that strange tongue I had sometimes heard them use when no one else was around. Phoenician? Aramaic? Some dialect from the eastern Mediterranean that existed in philological textbooks and nowhere else? I sometimes wondered where they had met, in what land and under what circumstances, and whether they had sat together with her mother and sisters, sipping tea beneath date palms in a shade-filled courtyard, while the fathers and uncles argued over her bride price. Such an unoriginal scenario seemed to me unlikely, however, and I hoped that one day I might be told the true story.

She had appeared at his side, her dark hair hidden beneath a shawl that hung below her waist, and her lips and dress were the colour of a ruby-red oleander. Bright gold shone from her ears and around her throat, and on her feet were the silver satin slippers she always wore whenever I visited them. She nodded agreement to whatever he had said and slipped away into the ship's interior.

I followed her with my eyes until a closing door hid her from view. She must be about twenty years younger than him, I thought, but she was one of those women whose faces reveal little about the length of time they have been lighting up dull rooms and catching the stray looks of strangers. And how old was he? The husband whose wishes she seemed to obey, without ever giving the impression of subservience, as though she had known beforehand that his instruction was the one she would have given herself. Possibly, some god or goddess knew his age; all I knew was that he was still strong and powerful as he strode along the deck, carrying ship's tackle as though it were child's play. His face was the face all sailors have, beaten bronze by exposure to wind and sun, the eyes clear and calculating. If pressed, I might have hazarded sixty, yet that seemed such a paltry number when you talked to him in the intimacy of his barge, surrounded by the books and photographs, the rolls of navigational charts; it seemed impossible that so much life could be crammed into such a brief frame of time, and when you stepped back onto the towpath on a late-autumn evening, with the yellow leaves drifting on the water below and the mumble of distant traffic reminding you of the civilisation you were returning to, you carried the sense of having passed time with a man whose life stretched back impossibly into the past, into a remoteness you could only guess at, in which, as the captain of a Phoenician sailing ship, he had steered his red-and-white-sailed boat into every port of the old Mediterranean, buying gold and silver in Iberia in exchange for oil and wine, and always looking for that extra margin of a profit that would enable him, not to retire to a white-walled house in a quiet street beyond the wash of the waves, but that would give him the means to buy a larger, more beautiful boat.

He was looking at his watch. 'It will soon be time to cast off,' he said. 'Better get some steam up.'

I collected my thoughts. 'The New Year Special?' I asked.

He smiled. 'Of course. What else could we use?'

That was another of our rituals that Phelbas had convinced me of. And if you have ever crossed the Bosphorus or sailed up the Golden Horn, like the *Astarte* herself, and as I myself had done in the days before the Bank, I am sure you too would have been entranced by the coils of black smoke curling from the funnels of the ferries as they chugged through the choppy grey waters, loaded with their cargoes of passengers. And especially down by the old Galata Bridge, where the fish sellers shouted for your custom and the smell of freshly fried mackerel drifted over the water; down there, if you lifted your eyes to the west, the sun already sunk from the smoky sky, you would hear the faithful being called to their twilit prayers from minaret after minaret, and see the entrance to the covered bazaar and those extraordinary mosques rising up the hill towards… towards Allah himself, I suppose. But I am digressing. It was the coal I wanted to tell you about.

For half a century it has been illegal to burn coal in the city of London, or any other British city for that matter, but for Phelbas, smokeless fuel was a substance both characterless and unnatural, and while he would tolerate its use on every other day, on this one trip, in the darkness of the old year, he would have his crew load a consignment of the rich, black stuff onto the boat, which would then be used to fire the furnace as we slipped our moorings and headed downstream. It was another bond between us, because no one else knew except Elyssa and the crew. Once the boat was under way, the two of us would stand in the stern, straining to see, or else imagining, the swathes of thick smoke rising from the funnel and spreading out like banners across the city. We, who were accustomed to the acrid smell, could inhale it like a drug, while the others, my colleagues, either failed to notice the change in the air or simply went inside, disliking the exposure to the darkly burning minerals. At such moments we would exchange a smile, locked in the smoky mystery of our secret.

The Bank's invitation-only, New Year's Eve Thames cruise and dinner was scheduled to cast off at 7.30, with the three-course meal (wine extra) being served from about 8.30. Phelbas would steam at a leisurely pace to Greenwich, where he would moor the boat until dinner was over. Then, instead of swinging round and heading back towards our point of departure, which was what most tourists did, the Phoenician would continue downstream for about another hour, passing between the open jaws of the Thames Barrier and over the Woolwich Tunnel, until, sometime before the first New Year rockets illuminated the sky, he would turn the boat across the width of the ever-broadening river and beat back towards the City, either with or against the current, depending on the state of the tide.

And at some point when the meal was over, as tradition decreed, someone would tell a story; something witty and not too long. In recent years, Henley had performed this task, much to my relief, as I dreaded the day when there would be no more volunteers.

I was about to go to the bar to get myself a drink before my colleagues started to arrive, when I heard my name being called from further along the deck. I turned and walked back to the gangplank to find Elyssa with two new passengers. She raised her face towards mine with a look of concern and glanced at the couple, who were standing beside her. I saw at once the nature of the problem. They were both dressed warmly against the river's clammy cold, but gloves, scarf and even a coat with a deep hood could not conceal the gender of one of them.

'Good evening, sir.'

The male – Lovell or Lovett, I think his name was – appeared to be dressed for the occasion, his dark coat covering what looked to be dinner jacket and black tie. You must understand there were no rules that had to be observed for the New Year's Eve cruise, except for the one about female participation, but those who had been before accepted that a degree of formality was implicit, was part of the tradition, was what the Directors expected from their staff.

And the Directors themselves? What would their role be as the evening unfolded? Because they would certainly be in attendance. Perhaps those of you who do not know me are under the impression that I myself have some special relationship to that select band, whose offices on the highest floor, accessible only by personal, leather-lined lift, gaze blankly across the city. I am afraid I must disappoint you, however. My own position, as I have mentioned, is not so exalted and only my long years of employment and a remote family connection to the Bank's founder have prevented the axe from falling on my vulnerable neck.

But Lovett, as I now remembered his name was, had more to say.

'I hope you don't mind me bringing my cousin this evening, sir. You see, she's staying with me at the moment – and I couldn't really leave her in the house on New Year's Eve, could I?' The brief speech stuttered to a halt and his uncertain manner left me doubting whether it was entirely true. He lowered his voice as if this were some sort of conspiracy. 'I mean, I realise it's against the rules—'

Which was the opening I had been looking for, especially as I could hear male voices from the quayside.

'That's just the point, Lovett—'

'Lovell,' he corrected.

'Sorry. Lovell. I'm afraid it's out of the question. There will be a lot of trouble if I permit your cousin to stay, when the women in the office were not invited.'

'I know all that, sir, but this is a special case, don't you think?'

'I can't allow any special cases,' I said, recoiling a little at the sound of my own voice. I glanced at the woman beside him, her arm through his, her face shadowed by the hood of her coat that was open at the throat, revealing a pale green silken scarf.

I could hear footsteps on the gangplank, and I knew if I let her remain the credibility of the evening would vanish. Someone touched my elbow and I turned to see Elyssa indicating she wished to speak to me. I bent my head, but she moved a few paces away from the others. I followed her.

'She could help serve the food,' Elyssa whispered. 'That wouldn't interfere with the rule. And then later, she could sit with me and listen to the after-dinner entertainment, those far-fetched stories Mr Henley always seems to tell.'

Her eyes looked into my own. There was a softness, but also a steeliness of purpose hidden within that gaze. *Think carefully*, they seemed to say, *before you decide*.

'All right,' I said. 'Let's see what she thinks of the idea.'

Elyssa smiled. 'Let me talk to her. I'm sure she'll agree.'

And agree she did, with the result that within a matter of moments, Lovell and I found ourselves without female company. I stared at him with new interest. He could not have been more than about twenty-five, with fair hair and very fine features. He wore gold-rimmed glasses and there was something of the academic about him; with his delicate fingers he looked as though he were more used to turning the pages of old manuscripts than counting currencies, so that I wondered if he was employed by the Bank in the library that occupied almost the whole of one floor, and passed his work-hours researching its history, which stretched backwards to the very invention of modern banking in Venice or Florence, I forget which; and then still further into the past to times before the moneylenders in Solomon's temple, to the merchants who made their loans in grains of primitive wheat in ancient Phoenicia. Or, at least, that's the story the Librarian, a slight, insubstantial woman who seemed to drift between the stacks of books like a husk blown from that same winnowed wheat, had once assured me.

'You said your companion is your cousin?'

'A very distant one,' he said, his air of discomfort returning. He looked at me gratefully. 'Thank you, sir. I appreciate the gesture very much indeed.'

And so it was that later, after the moment that always resonates when the gangplank is hauled on board and the mooring rope flung in coils upon the deck, and the sensation of a voyage commencing hums in the blood like a half-remembered tune; after Phelbas had started the engine with a shudder that shook the boat from stem to stern, and I had inhaled that first lungful of smoke-tinged air from the funnel and we began to move out into midstream; after I had made my way from face to well-scrubbed face in the crush around the bar and greeted as many of the sixty or so colleagues who had arrived as I could, as though our relationship was based on something more enduring than a shared place of employment; after the *Astarte* had steamed downriver through the dark before docking at Greenwich and we had all sat down to eat in the dining saloon, to be waited on by Elyssa and Lovell's beguiling distant cousin (now without her coat and wearing an apron to protect her evening dress), or by members of the crew, press-ganged for the occasion, who would clearly have been happier shovelling coal or hauling ropes than pouring wine and serving fish; after all this, I say, with wet lips wiped and stomachs full of the food the caterers had provided, cigar smoke hanging in a blue haze above our heads (this was, after all, a private function), they sat waiting, expectancy stirring, faces turned in my direction, so that I knew the moment had arrived to tap my wine glass, to patter out my trite words to the Directors, sitting together at the head of one of the long tables, and to the company in general, before asking if anyone had a story to while away the time until we cast off and Phelbas steered us towards our furthest point from the City, from what one might call home.

And after a moment's silence, in which my eyes roamed the tables for someone who might accept the challenge, it was Henley, with a professional's practised cough, who glanced in my direction and gave his familiar opening: 'Well, if no one else wishes to hold forth, I do happen to have something that might interest one or two of you, on a night such as this.'

At which, naturally enough, there were cries of, 'Surely not' and 'But we heard it last year', et cetera, yet I was sure that those who had been before had been waiting for this, for old Henley's cough and the sight of him getting to his feet, beer glass in one hand, cigar in the other, not quite able to conceal his pleasure.

He glanced around the table and, with a nod, acknowledged the Directors, but I knew that the story he was going to tell was not for them, and that was one of the reasons why I liked him. He must have been nearly eighty and pensioned off years ago, yet the details of his life were a mystery. For reasons I could not explain, my department had no file on him, yet everyone knew him by sight. I had no idea if he still had an office or what it was that he did, but he appeared invulnerable to the vicissitudes of banking life, and behaved accordingly. Sometimes, in a bar on Lower Thames Street on a Friday after work, you heard extravagant tales about his younger days, which you could not believe, because they did not match the upright figure standing before us who, in his manner and speech, and his opinions when he offered them, seemed to be older than old school. Irrespective of Bank policy, he went his own way. The script he read from was his own, and he never paid for the evening; as though he considered his skills as raconteur and troubadour to be payment enough. (The Bank, ungenerous by nature, did not invite its employees to occasions such as these, though our presence was expected and repeated absence would be noted in the records it was popularly believed were kept on all of us.)

With a faint smile, Henley emptied his glass and replaced it on the table. He didn't seem to drink wine or spirits. Despite his thinning hair and the long years behind him, he was a tall, imposing figure in his white shirt and dark suit, whose jacket sleeves were shiny from service. He never wore a dinner jacket.

'A dry throat's no use at all for what I'm about to tell you,' he said. He put the cigar to his lips and inhaled deeply before breathing the smoke out above our heads. The chatter had died down. No cutlery clinked; no chairs scraped. I caught sight of Elyssa and Lovell's cousin sitting away to my right, their bright dresses alive against the sombre colours of the males around them. Henley cleared his throat.

'I suppose those of you with any education will have heard of the Siege of Troy.'

'Don't tell us you were there, Henley,' someone muttered.

Henley took the banter for granted. Audience participation was part of his performance; a part of the ritual. 'In spirit, maybe.'

'But on whose side?'

'The losers', naturally.' He looked round at us. 'Learning how to take the knocks life dishes out seems to be what matters most as you get older.'

'Don't you mean kicks?' someone called Beddoes, who saw himself as the Bank's joker, put in. 'It was a horse, remember. The Trojan one.'

There were groans, but Henley rode them with ease.

'Those refugee Trojans, led by Aeneas,' he went on, 'founded kingdoms all over Europe, and one among them, a legendary figure called Felix Brutus, set sail for these shores and founded the kingdom on whose green pastures we now walk.'

There were mutterings about the Last Night of the Proms, but Henley ignored them.

'I mention all this by way of a preamble, if I may use that word.' He smiled at the ironic nods around the table. 'I mention it because the setting of the story I am going to tell reminds me of that man's descendant, King Arthur, and his Knights of the Round Table, who were fortunate to live in a time when truth and loyalty and promise-keeping were the greatest virtues.' He paused to survey us with what I took to be a rather mocking sweep of his eyes. 'And chastity, too – though I suspect some of you have never heard of the word.'

Predictable, scurrilous uproar, during which I glanced across at our two lady companions to see how they were coping with the rowdy male audience they found themselves among. They seemed to be enjoying themselves.

Henley stood there while the uproar continued, a smile on his lips, and I had the strange feeling he had been saving the story he was about to tell for tonight, as if his almost mythical status at the Bank was based on a history he had always carried with him, and now the time had arrived for us all to hear it.

'It was a night like tonight, a New Year's Eve within living memory. A bankers' banquet in the great dining hall of a mansion that had managed to survive the Blitz.'

He had not raised his voice to create the space he needed for his words. The story itself had done that. Once again, he had our attention; the preliminary skirmishes were over and the tale Henley had kept for this occasion would make itself heard.

'What you have to imagine are rows of tables in a hall far larger than this, and on a raised platform – a dais, you might wish to call it – was the top table, at which the managers of this particular bank and their special guests were all seated.'

'Why don't you tell us the name of the bank, Henley?'

'Because the name's not important. It could be any bank.'

'But you know it. I'm sure you do. It's our Bank, isn't it?

'Stop interrupting. Let the man tell his story.'

A sheepish silence, and I looked round for the authoritative owner of the last voice.

'The meal was done, and the debris cleared away by the servants. Spirits were being served and cigars lit. I suspect there would have been no cigars at Camelot, but otherwise the scene was very similar.' Henley gave us another of his dry looks. 'And in the character of the guests gathered to celebrate the arrival of another New Year, I doubt one would have noticed any real difference to us either; though we are sat in this pleasure steamer's small saloon, with the cold and murky waters beneath us and the City we are all so familiar with, lost behind a bend in the river.'

He paused, and I leaned forward in my seat, so I could see him better. I was struck by the style of delivery he had slipped into, but I noticed also a sombreness in his voice that had not been present in any of the previous tales he had told us over the years.

'I don't know what time it was – there was a clock high on one of the walls, among the paintings and tapestries that spoke of the hall's illustrious past, but I cannot recall the position of the hands—'

'Are you telling us you were present at this meal, Henley?' a fund manager with thin lips, who had interrupted before, wanted to know.

'I think it's a story,' the man with the authoritative voice said sarcastically, and as I tried to identify the speaker, I recalled reading as a student about Charles Darwin's colleague – I could no longer remember his name – who had defended his friend's theory of evolution so vigorously in public debate that he had acquired the nickname of the Bulldog. It seemed an appropriate name for Henley's unknown champion.

'Some after-dinner entertainment was expected,' Henley continued; 'a recital of some kind, perhaps a story or two, but at the moment when an unspoken consensus seemed to have decided that this was the time for something to take place, there was a roar from outside, the oak doors to the hall burst open, and a motorcycle thundered up the central aisle to stop, the rear tyre squealing, in front of those seated at the top table.

'Of course, you can imagine the commotion: people on their feet, cries of amazement, even the odd scream – there were ladies present at this occasion – but there was also a sense of paralysis. As though all of us watching were powerless to prevent whatever was about to unfold. For that something frightful was going to take place, there seemed no doubt.

'The rider twisted the grip in his hand to rev the engine to its fullest and fill the hall with a cloud of exhaust fumes and the machine's infernal roar. Then, with a flick of his fingers he silenced the beast and, rising up from the saddle, lifted the visor of his helmet to survey us. A hush fell upon the hall. He was like a figure from a dreadful dream.

'Everything about him was green. Each garment he wore – jacket, trousers, gauntlets and boots – was a different shade of emerald green. He was a giant of a man, who handled the motorcycle he sat astride as though it were a child's first bicycle. He must have been at least seven feet tall, with a broad chest and arms and thighs that seemed to be bursting through the green leather that contained them. Below the helmet, a green beard spread across his leather jacket.'

Henley paused to look round the saloon.

'Strapped across his back, its handle sheathed in a green leather case, its blade gleaming in the light from the chandeliers overhead, was an enormous axe.'

A green man? It did seem a little unlikely. I heard a flurry of murmuring and saw that a note was being passed from hand to hand in Henley's direction. He accepted it from the final recipient and, after taking a pair of reading glasses from his pocket, unfolded the paper and glanced over it. Somewhere, someone among the listeners could not contain a snigger.

'Just a little joke, Henley.'

Henley looked briefly towards the speaker and then commenced to read out loud: '*Dear Mr Henley, would you be so kind to inform us as to the make and model of said motorcycle? I am an enthusiast, you see. Yours, etc.*'

Replacing the glasses in his pocket, Henley appeared to be considering his response. 'Not an entirely idle question, Dawkins, though it is customary to attach one's name to communications of this kind.' (A ripple of laughter.) 'Such details as you have requested tend to clog up the flow of the tale, which is why I omitted them. But as you seem so keen to know, I can tell you it was a Norton, something like a 650, I expect. A very powerful beast indeed.'

From my seat, I could observe Henley's face without difficulty, and once again I was struck by the seriousness of purpose that was present in his story this evening, even in the dry tones he used to respond to such a facetious question.

'Dismounting from his machine and securing it on its stand, this green rider removed his helmet and hung it from the handlebars. His face was broad and what little skin was visible beneath his beard was browned by the sun, as though even in the dead of winter, the man lived outdoors. Then he stepped onto the dais where the high table stood, and, indifferent to the powerful positions and reputations of those beside him, he started to address us. And of course, no boy's squeaky voice emerged from such a throat. His words stretched out towards the rafters.

"'Greetings. Do not be disturbed by my appearance or the manner of my arrival here." He paused, turning his head from one side to the other, as though searching out the furthest recesses of the hall, as if to ascertain there was no one present who was not giving him their full attention. "This city, through whose streets I have ridden at speed in order to be here on time; the building in which you sit; this enormous room in which you have eaten and drunk to your hearts' content, are well known where I come from – a place I am sure none of you have ever visited."

'The words rolled around the hall, breaking and echoing against the panelled walls so that his accent defied me. His speech revealed neither class nor education, district or region. I could hear no trace of London or West Country; no Birmingham, Wales, Lancashire, Liverpool, Manchester or Yorkshire; no Geordie; no Scots or Irish, or even, far over the Atlantic, American, in the sound of anything he said. He seemed to have come from somewhere that was neither north or south, west or east, but rather an unplaceable in-between land that occupied an indefinable location at the very centre of this island.

"'Because of this lack of reciprocity, I thought I would come here tonight to throw down a challenge – to anyone bold enough to accept the terms I offer." He paused to cast his eyes over his audience once more. "You are men of finance, bankers who make your money by shuffling papers and fumbling documents across littered tables, while the rest of the world works to provide you with the counters you play with."

'If the hall had been quiet before, a deep silence prevailed now, and I sensed a mounting anger at the way we were having to listen to this man's insults.

'"How the devil did you manage to get in here?" a guest who had risen from his seat cried out.

'"Like any other honest citizen, I came through the door," the green man replied. "But if you are upset by my bad manners, by my presumption, I suggest you wait to discover the nature of the challenge I am about to make. Then, if you have the courage of your convictions, you can accept my terms and strive to earn the prize – in your language, the profit – that I offer. If you prevail, you will have your revenge on me."

'He turned away from the heckler and, reaching into the motorcycle's saddlebags, he produced a block of wood, which he placed on the ground, and then a rectangular object wrapped in what looked like pale silk. With a magician's flourish, as if this was the promised entertainment, he stripped the object bare and left us gazing at a bar of gold. A faint sigh was squeezed from the hundreds of guests; a feeling of collective covetousness, I suspect, that was almost tangible. The figure on the dais nodded. "I thought you would find the reward appealing," he said.

'He blew on the ingot he held in one hand and rubbed it with the cloth, before offering it for inspection to those seated at the top table. "Is this fool's gold?" I heard him ask, and, by way of reply, he received a cursory shake of the head. Then, taking the bar once more, he placed it on the block of wood he had stood on end. In one swift movement, he reached behind him and drew the axe from its sheath.

Raising it high above his head, he brought it crashing down with a hiss, cleaving air, gold and the block of wood, before the blade buried itself in the floor. All around the hall people rose to their feet in alarm, or even panic, at what they had witnessed. Some were making their way towards the doors at the rear. The managers and their important guests were standing and had backed away from the fearsome figure before them, who, seeing the uproar he had caused, held up the two halves of the gold bar.

'"You cannot leave the hall!" he roared. "Go back to your seats, or are you really so spineless that the sight of a man with an axe frightens you half to death?!"

'"There are ladies present," a voice called.

'"Then let them go if what I say terrifies them so much. And may God help their children."

'His ringing tones had the desired effect, and I watched as people, muttering to each other, started to return to their seats and sit down again. I glanced towards the doors through which he had ridden and saw that they remained closed. No one, not even the most timid of the ladies, had been prepared to confirm his contemptuous opinion of us and accept his offer to leave.

'"I shall not keep you much longer," he said, as the hall fell into silence once more. "You will all be free to continue your conversations, or escape to your homes in the suburbs once you have heard me out." He paused. "But I hope there will be one brave soul among you willing to take up my challenge."

'"What if the brave soul happens to be one of your spineless women?" a female voice called out. "Or is the so-called fairer sex barred by some small print from taking part?"

'There were a few cries of "Bravo!" at this interjection, but the man on the dais laughed at her question.

'"I would be honoured to face such a challenger. There are no rules that would deny her. But I would have to wonder at the mettle of the men in this hall who would be content to flounder in her wake, clinging like children to the hem of her gown."'

I found myself marvelling at Henley's descriptions, the dialogue, the literary language, the variety of voices he used to project his characters; indeed, the entire nature of the story he was telling. He must have spent a long time rehearsing this performance.

'I could hear angry whispers among the men,' Henley continued, 'and I began to wonder if the green figure had the power to hold us in our seats while he continued to mock us. He was occupied, however, with what I presumed would be the final presentation of his challenge, the exact nature of which remained a mystery. He had placed a pair of scales on the top table, and in each weighing pan he had laid one half of the gold bar. He had asked one of the managers to examine the weight, I presumed, for we heard him say, "Tell them what you have just seen with your own eyes." The dinner-jacketed figure was clearly unused to being told what to do, however, and remained seated, staring silently towards the rear of the hall. The green man leaned towards him and said something. The result was immediate, for the manager was abruptly on his feet and speaking in an uncertain voice:

'"Our uninvited guest has asked me to point out" – a word in his ear made him change the verb – "to confirm, that the two halves of this gold bar are of exactly equal weight."'

'Seems a bit far-fetched,' someone on the table near me, who had still not finished eating and had a spoonful of trifle in his hand, said. 'I mean, to split the bar into two identical halves. With an axe…' He looked around, as if to seek support for his opinion, but Henley chose to ignore him, continuing his story in the voice of the green intruder.

'"Tell them the amount."'

'"Each half weighs twenty-five troy ounces."'

'So what was that worth then, Henley?' This voice belonged to the sceptical fund manager seated by the window who had interrupted on a number of occasions. 'Assuming that "then" is a fixed point in time and not a fictitious location in your devious mind.'

'Historical gold prices are not my speciality, I'm afraid,' Henley answered, taking the opportunity to have a sip of beer. He had succeeded, as he always did, in tying each colleague in the threads of his story. I glanced at their attentive faces. No one was playing with his phone or looking at his watch and I wondered what the two women were making of it all. Elyssa had sat through Henley's performances before, but his previous tales had been light in tone and more anecdotal, rooted in a world of markets and currencies we were familiar with. The story he was telling this evening was of a different order altogether and I doubted that its conclusion, which seemed hidden and faraway – was he intending to tell a second instalment next year, I wondered? – would possess the dry, humorous punchline appropriate to an occasion like this, and which he usually delivered with such panache.

And the girl sitting at Elyssa's side; Lovell's 'distant cousin'? Though she was no longer wearing the hooded coat, so the red-gold hair coiled at the back of her head was visible, she retained an air of mystery and her long, pale green evening dress was like the outer leaves of a slender plant from which her body would emerge in the spring. Among this crowd of men, the two women, so different in appearance, sparkled like jewels. In her red dress, with her black ringlets and olive skin, Elyssa could have been painted on a Minoan vase, while her companion, her skin like milk, might have arrived on the *Astarte* from a fairy tale set in some northern forest, where wolves howl through the long winter nights.

'On today's market, the whole bar would be worth about fifty thousand in sterling.' It was one of the Directors who was speaking. 'I also have no idea what it would have been worth at the time these events take place, which Mr Henley has not specified, but it would have been a tidy sum.'

'Yes, a tidy sum,' Henley repeated with the flicker of a smile and without turning his head towards the source of the information.

'"To the man, or woman,"' he went on, in the green man's words, '"who accepts the challenge, I will give this half-bar of fourteen-carat gold. It will be theirs to invest as they see fit for a year and a day. When that time has elapsed, on that very day, it will be their sworn duty to search me out to discover who has been the more successful trader, for I will have invested the other half." He paused to draw breath, to let his terms sink in. "Whoever has made the most profit keeps everything – the value of both halves of the ingot, as well as the proceeds made by both parties."

'"Why are you doing this? I mean, what exactly is in it for you?"

'The figure on the dais, still holding both halves of the gold bar he had spliced so cleanly, so perfectly, in two, looked at the grey-haired speaker seated in front of him, as if he had been expecting the question.

'"You might say I am a man who cannot resist a challenge, especially one that I know I will win."

'The speaker had risen to his feet; his voice too rang around the hall, and I had the impression he was speaking for everyone who was angered by the green man's behaviour.

'"Setting aside for a moment the arrogance you have displayed in interrupting our festivities tonight and, uninvited, addressing this gathering in such a scandalous manner, there is one thing I do not understand. Even assuming someone here is fool enough to take up your so-called challenge, what would prevent him from absconding with his half of the gold? Why should he take the trouble to find you? What would make him want to even bother? Everything about your behaviour suggests you are operating outside the law, so I think it unlikely you would be able to enforce your rules for this challenge in any court. I mean," and he glanced to either side to include the rest of us in his observation, "I can't honestly see the British police coming to your assistance in such circumstances."

'There was laughter, and for the first time it seemed that the intruder had overreached himself. The speaker took a few steps closer to the dais.

"'I would happily accept your challenge myself on the terms so far mentioned – were it not for the fact that I suspect there is a catch you are concealing from us."

'And folding his arms, as though he now had charge of the proceedings, he stood waiting, as were we all, to hear what the green man would have to say. There was a round of applause and two of the managers themselves stood up to congratulate him. The mood in the hall had changed and it seemed as though the braggart on the dais would have to admit defeat, returning to whatever godforsaken place he came from, soundly beaten and with his tail between his legs. But when I glanced at the expression on the green man's face, I saw that things might not turn out as simply as that. He too took a pace forward and stepped down from the dais to confront his challenger; they would even have been standing face to face, were it not for the fact that the green man towered head and shoulders above the other fellow.

"'You are, of course, correct. I would be a fool to come to such a gathering as this expecting good faith and honesty. And because I have no reason to trust you, not even the ladies scattered around the tables" – I thought I heard someone hiss at this point – "I will demand something from whoever it is who takes his half of the gold bar. You might well call this a catch; I prefer to call it a surety, a bond of good faith from whoever accepts the challenge."

"'I'll take your gold and the challenge too, you loud-mouthed clown. How much is this bond you demand?" A younger guest, wallet in hand, was on his feet now. He was of similar, if somewhat smaller, proportions to the intruder, and possessed the same barrel-like chest, the same sense of muscles stretching to breaking point the seams of his formal evening wear; and his hands looked as though they should have been hacking coal from a seam underground. His manner of speech lacked refinement, and it was difficult to imagine him spending his days behind the counter of a bank in the City or in the office. The green man remained unmoved by this new, more aggressive response.

'"The surety is one of faith, not cash, sir. All that is required of you is the courage to strike a blow with this axe on my bent neck. You may rest assured I shall not resist you. Then, a year and a day from now, you must bow your head to receive the same from me." He stared hard into the eyes of the bull-like figure to see if he was still so sure of himself. "This blow will, however, be waived in the event that you have made more profit from investing your half of the gold than myself." There was a pause as the green man waited to allow the implications of the challenge to sink into the minds of everyone present.

'"If, on the other hand, you should think to cheat me, be warned that I shall not rest until I have found you, and the blow I shall deliver with this axe" – he turned to wrench the weapon from the floor – "will be such as not one of you has ever witnessed."

'There was a moment when it seemed as though each of the two guests on their feet was seriously considering becoming involved in such lunacy, but then, with shakes of the head, they both sat down.

'"I think it might be a good idea if someone called the police," the grey-haired banker said loudly and to no one in particular. "Our friend here is obviously off his head."

'The mood in the hall appeared to be in the balance. There must have been over two hundred people still awaiting the arrival of the New Year, yet all were gripped by the unfolding drama. I heard one or two ladies crying softly, but behind us the doors remained shut. No one took up the suggestion of going to telephone the police.' Henley looked at his attentive listeners. 'I trust no one needs reminding these were the days before mobile phones. Everyone present seemed transfixed by the commanding presence of the green man, who had returned to the dais. On the table behind him, where the managers sat, impotently observing these events, the two halves of the gold bar waited like unclaimed brides; and in the eerie almost-silence, dressed from head to toe in emerald-green leather, his motorcycle waiting beside him like some patient beast, with the terrible axe gripped in his hands, he faced us with the challenge that I thought no one would be foolish enough to accept.

'"I see there is indeed no one," he said at length. "I half suspected that would be the case. I shall be forced to return home with my gold unclaimed and my opinion of you all confirmed."

'"Only a madman would take up your challenge," the grey-haired man said loudly. "I think you're witness to the good sense and responsibility of our profession, which you have disgracefully insulted."

'"Gutless and cowardly, is how I would describe the behaviour of all of you in this hall," the intruder responded. "Your sense of responsibility is simply an excuse for the failure to step out of your dark rooms and into the world beyond the counting tables where you spend your days. Not one of you is prepared to risk something of themselves, to be alive in their own flesh and blood. You are all wretched creatures, not worth my interest in you, not worthy of life."

'His words sounded like a half-crazed ranter's on a street corner somewhere, high on alcohol or some god or other, but at the same time, strangely, they fell through the air like stuff which could be sifted for meaning, or at least that's how it seemed to me.

'And then a voice from somewhere deep in the corners of the room; a voice whose words did not seem credible. A chair scraped, and people were turning their heads, craning their necks to catch sight of whoever had spoken and was on their feet. Whisperings took wing and fluttered round the hall.

'"I accept the challenge on the terms you offer."

'People were reaching out to this fellow to try and hold him back, but like everything else that had happened this evening, events were unfolding with a logic of their own, which no one appeared able to prevent. And so it was that, a few moments later, the challenger was standing on the dais before the green stranger.

'"Go back to your seat, you fool!" someone shouted.

'One of the managers was on his feet, leaning forward in an attempt to dissuade the newcomer, but his mind appeared made up. Dressed like every other male guest in dinner jacket and black tie, he seemed completely nondescript. His hair was neither dark nor fair, his features in no way memorable, and though he was tall, his build did not seem that of someone prepared to wield a monstrous axe in a few minutes' time. Perhaps the sole thing that struck one was the sense of resolution that filled him.'

Henley stopped speaking. I assumed he needed a drink or wanted a breather, but he just stood there, swaying slightly as if the boat was moving beneath him, which it wasn't, as we were still firmly moored to the quay at Greenwich. He looked in danger of losing his balance, and I saw him grip the back of his chair.

'I say, Henley, are you all right?' someone beside him asked.

He nodded. 'Just needed to catch my breath there for a second,' he said shakily, reaching for his glass. I followed his actions anxiously, as I'm sure everyone else did. He took a long drink and straightened up.

'Sorry about that. I don't know what came over me.' He drew a deep breath, closed his eyes and began to speak, and we were back in that hall again on that other New Year's Eve.

'The green stranger bowed – whether in irony or not was hard to tell – and they stood facing each other on the dais, their heights strikingly unequal.

'"If you accept the challenge, you must tell me your name," the green man said.

'"I don't think any of us has heard yours yet."

'It was a spirited response, and drew a murmur of approval from the guests who were following these developments with the kind of dread I suppose was once felt at public executions.

'The stranger stared at his challenger for a moment before reaching into a pocket and pulling out what looked like a business card, which he laid on the table behind them. "Very well. You will be able to discover who I am after you have struck your blow. Provided you have the courage you say you have."

'But though the green man did not seem to have heard it, the challenger's identity, like the name of some legendary hero, was being whispered among those seated around me.

'"My name is Gavin," the young man announced, in a voice that sounded remarkably calm. "I come from an old family and am not afraid to reveal it."

'And all this while, the managers sat there, powerless to intervene in the events that were unfolding a few feet in front of them. The young man looked up at the stranger and held out his arm to take the axe.

'"I think everyone is waiting."

'There was silence in the hall. Not a glass clinked, not a knife scraped against a plate. Breathing itself appeared to have ceased.

'"You understand what you are committing yourself to?" the green man responded.

'"Perfectly, in the terms you have explained."

'For a few moments, the green man looked his young challenger in the eye. He had mocked what he called our lack of courage, but now that someone stood ready to perform his bidding, was he having second thoughts? The air around the two figures seemed thin and empty, and it felt as if each one of us sat within the range of that terrible axe. Then, with a curt nod, the green-clad stranger tossed the axe to the other who, caught off guard, struggled to hold it and maintain his balance at the same time. The stranger knelt.

'"May the truer man win," he said, and bowed his head to receive the blow.

'The challenger stood there and we waited for him to come to his senses; for the police or doctors in white coats, brandishing syringes and carrying a straitjacket, to arrive, or simply for someone to get up on the dais and prevent him from attempting what he appeared set on doing. But none of these things happened. As I said before, a kind of powerlessness seemed to fill us all.'

'Henley, I need to get this straight. No evasions, please. Are you saying this is a true story? Are you telling us you were there?' There was a pause. 'Is that you why you went a bit strange, because telling this story has made it all come back to you?'

It was the mistrustful voice from earlier and, in my mind, he was no longer some annoying fund manager obsessed with graphs and data as manifestations of the market, but the Interrupter, whose initial letter was written large.

'You keep saying, "I" all the time,' the trifle-eater added.

'It's a narrative device,' I broke in, irritated by the interruptions. 'Henley has a first-person narrator to bring the story to life. It doesn't literally mean he was present.'

There was some muttering. I suppose I sounded pompous, but the general ignorance, despite the huge salaries and bonuses some of them earned, annoyed me.

Henley glanced in my direction and then, to my astonishment, said, 'As far as I'm concerned, the story is true. I even have a token, a bit of evidence, I suppose you might call it, that I can show you later if any of you are interested.'

Some of them were, but the main preoccupation, mine included, was to find out what was going to happen next.

'For a few seconds Gavin hefted the axe in his hands, getting a feel for its centre of gravity. Then, leaning it against the table, he removed his jacket. The green stranger looked up, but on seeing Gavin pick the axe up again, he bowed his head once more. The young man shifted his balance from one foot to the other like someone preparing to take a golf swing, and the thought struck me that maybe this was his sole training for the task he was about to perform. He raised the great axe above his head and above the figure of the green man, kneeling, neck laid bare, before him, and I could feel a cry rising in my throat and perhaps in the throats of all who found themselves compelled to watch. The axe fell like a bolt from heaven, ripping the air and biting through flesh and bone. There were frightful screams, both male and female, as the severed head dropped and bounced like a ghastly football towards the first table. It was like a scene from a macabre, blackly comic film as guests kicked it away from them and fell over their chairs in their efforts to scramble out of the way. Now there was, finally, pandemonium. The doors were thrown open at the back and I could hear people crying and screaming, desperate to escape the hall. A lady nearby was sick into her handbag, while her male companion, open-mouthed, stared towards the headless figure upon the dais, from which a spurt of blood had briefly fountained. I too gazed in that direction and watched in horror as the trunk, its bodily functions unimpaired, the blood flow staunched, stepped down to retrieve what it had lost from under the nearest table. Holding it by its long, green hair, the maimed stranger, his green leather now splashed with drops of crimson blood, climbed back onto the dais and directed the gaze of his detached head towards the face of the man who had beheaded him.

'"Be wise enough, sir – or perhaps, Sir Gavin, I should call you. Be wise enough to keep your word and remember the terms of our contract. I shall be waiting for you in a year and a day to return this blow you have given me – unless the profit from your half of the gold is greater than mine. Do not fail me," he said. "If you search honestly, you will find me at the Green Chapel."

'Prising the axe from the other's grip, he replaced it in the sheath on his back. He took one half of the gold bar from the managers' table, only one of whom remained to witness these final acts, and pushed it back into a saddlebag. Then, holding his head in one hand, he started the engine with a kick of his green-booted foot, jumped astride the machine and, wheeling it around, roared back down the aisle, the remaining guests stumbling and falling behind him like scavenging gulls tossed in the wake of a pleasure steamer, as it heads towards the open sea.'

The Journey

Henley surveyed our faces for a moment and sat down. There was a silence, followed by a burst of applause. As he turned to me, I gave an appreciative nod, despite being taken aback by the nature of his performance. Even with my undistinguished literary background I recognised the source, but I was not sure why Henley had turned a medieval poem about one of King Arthur's knights into a story set in the recent past, or why he wanted to give the impression he was present at the New Year's Eve banquet he had described. The undertaking, if successful, would take hours to accomplish. I recalled his final words before he sat down: the comparison of the guests being tossed in the wake of the headless motorcyclist to seagulls; the simile, though not particularly original, was literary in nature and seemed to belong to a written text, not an oral, after-dinner entertainment. Had Henley written this new version down? Surely he hadn't learned it by heart? I shook my head in bafflement.

Voices were calling from different corners of the dining saloon and I could see that Phelbas had appeared in the doorway.

'But what about the rest, Henley? You only seem to have given us the first part. Surely you don't expect us to hang around till next year to hear the conclusion?' The speaker – it was Beddoes again – glanced round the table. 'Judging by this year's financial results, some of us might not get invitations then.'

The joke fell flat, but there was a growing clamour in which Henley's name could clearly be heard. Henley himself had accepted another glass of beer from someone and was drinking the contents slowly, seemingly unperturbed by the tumult going on around him. His cigar had gone out while he had been speaking, and I saw him reach for his lighter to rekindle it. Despite the adulation, there was a quality of aloneness about him that the calls for more could not dispel. I knew from casual conversations that he had never married and carried with him the air of the eternal bachelor, but where was home, and which train, underground or suburban, would ferry him there in the early hours of the morning?

'We want the rest! We want the rest!' Voices were calling in ragged unison, as though they were back at their boys-only schools. And then they fell to chanting his name, softly at first, as if they were at a football match. 'Henley, Henley, Henley…'

His name swirled around the dining room like the incoming tide, growing in volume until it broke over our heads in a wave of sound. As the organiser of the evening, even the Captain, as Phelbas insisted on calling me, I realised I needed to do something, but I could not see how our schedule would permit a continuation, even if Henley had enough stamina to go on with the story. I saw he was in conversation with one of the guests who had been loudest in demanding he continue, and wondered if he had been prepared for this all along. Out of the corner of my eye, I saw Phelbas beckoning me from the doorway, so, getting to my feet, I left events to take care of themselves for a few minutes.

The Phoenician took me out on deck, where I found the sky had cleared enough for the pale-faced moon to gaze at us from behind the rags of cloud. The boat rocked at its moorings, and the river seemed in a hurry as it flowed past. I could hear loud voices from the saloon, though the chanting had ebbed away, and the sounds of music and people partying drifted towards us from Greenwich, and further upriver from the pubs of Deptford; the old haunt of that dead poet and playwright, Christopher Marlowe, stabbed in the eye in a fatal brawl over the bill. The wash of the water against the boat, the distant drunken shouting, sharpened this melancholy edge to my thoughts as I looked at Phelbas questioningly.

'I don't trust this calm, "all's well with the world" feeling,' he said. 'Weather reports aren't fairy tales.' He turned his face to the sea breeze and inhaled. 'The storms are out there, biding their time. They'll make themselves known when they're ready.'

Respecting his judgement, I nodded, wondering about storms that inhabited those mystical regions of the shipping forecast – Dogger, Fisher, German Bight, Humber and Thames – and which might consciously set out to deceive you, as if they lived lives of their own and were not random, natural phenomena; in the same way that the river, in Phelbas' mind, I supposed, kept its tricks hidden in its long, rippling sleeves. I told him that the storytelling might go on for longer than planned and asked if it might be possible to delay our departure. He frowned.

'You and I both like to have everyone on deck when we pass through the Barrier. It's the highlight of the evening, so it would be disappointing if the guests were still down below.' He looked at his watch. 'It'll soon be 10.30. We should not cast off later than eleven. They'll miss most of the fireworks, as we'll be back later than usual, that's all.'

'Let's do it that way,' I said. 'There'll be fireworks enough to see as we sail back up the river, and I feel sure the weather will be kind to us.' I looked at him. 'I'll do my best to have things over by then, but' – I shrugged – 'sometimes stories go on for longer than you expect.'

He nodded and turned to go, but I saw in his eye a look that said he would have preferred a different arrangement.

I knew it was important to return to the dining saloon quickly and convey what had been agreed, but I lingered to gaze up through the dark, towards the Observatory and its zero meridian, invisibly severing east from west, while close by on the hill, the collection of time pieces in the Maritime Museum ticked away the life of the world.

When I descended the stairs to the dining saloon, I found the door closed and, on opening it, that the clamour of my departure had been replaced by an atmosphere of quiet anticipation. It felt as though a conspiratorial agreement had been reached, which, for some reason, I would have attempted to hinder. I saw that wine and beer glasses had been replenished, ties loosened, and chairs moved to more advantageous positions. Faces turned towards me as I entered but, not wishing to disturb the proceedings, I gave Henley, who was on his feet again, a nod to confirm it was all right for him to continue. I tapped my watch and mouthed the word 'eleven' to him, which I hoped he understood. I didn't want to imagine the uproar there would have been if I'd tried to forestall the second part of his performance. I slipped into my place and sat back to listen.

It seemed I had missed nothing. Henley had not even commenced the preamble to the second part, which I suspected he had intended to deliver all along, and, though the story was compelling, I found it striking that he had managed to cast such a spell over so many of the Bank's employees, most of whom would be less than half his age. Even the Directors, in their splendid isolation at the head of their table, seemed to have offered no objections to the turn of events.

'This is the second instalment of my little tale,' he resumed. 'After this there will be no others.'

It was a curious thing to say. As if the conclusion to the story would also signify the end of Henley's role as storyteller on our New Year's Eve outings. I stared at him, but his face showed no sign of emotion. None of the other guests responded, though the words seemed to hang over us like a cloud of incense, heavy with a significance that would resist scientific interpretation.

'As I was saying before I sat down,' Henley resumed with a glance round the faces before him, 'and to assist those among you with memories already muddied by alcohol, the young hero, Gavin, had as good as signed a contract with the green-clad stranger who had ridden his motorcycle into the middle of a bank's New Year's Eve festivities and challenged someone to behead him with his enormous axe.'

'Please spare us a retelling of the details,' a voice whispered, though loud enough for all to hear.

'Of course,' Henley answered. 'As is customary, there is

a deadline to be observed – time's wingèd chariot, et cetera, et cetera – so I will remind you only of the terms of the contract itself, which can be summarised as follows: on New Year's Eve of the year following, Gavin must present himself at a place called the Green Chapel with his half of the gold ingot, newly smelted to contain whatever profit he has earned from investing its original value. If he has gained more than the stranger, he keeps both halves and the contract is fulfilled. If the stranger has won, however, not only must Gavin give up the gold, he must also bow his head to receive one blow from the axe. The consequence of which, presumably, will not be as miraculous as it was in the stranger's case.'

Henley paused, and I thought I could feel his audience urging him to turn the page and take us further. But, as always, there were those whose love of themselves would not give the storyteller the freedom he needed to tell his tale in his own fashion.

'"The Green Chapel" is not much to go on.'

'What about this green fellow's business card?' someone else asked. 'Didn't you say he left it on the table?'

Henley reached into the pocket of his jacket and held something up. 'This is what I promised to show you,' he said. 'It's the card the stranger left on the top table.'

There was a murmur of voices and I hoped I wasn't going to have to intervene with another unwanted explanation, even though this was not so much a narrative device as a dramatic one. I wished Henley would get on with it, but he was clearly enjoying himself.

'The intruder's card was a dark, glossy green, and looked

like a holly leaf with five points. It contained no address or phone number, just the name *Greneknighte* and the word *Privatier*.'

'What the fuck's a *privatier*?' someone nearby asked. 'I thought public sentiment wanted us to stop using all this European terminology.'

A few people laughed, but there were also murmurs of disapproval.

'Well done, my little piece of lowlife. Congratulations on your vocabulary. A pity you managed to forget how to behave in the presence of ladies,' the Bulldog growled.

'I couldn't agree more,' Henley said, raising his voice above the rumblings of discontent. 'In my view, courtesy has always been the chief characteristic of a civilised man.'

The uncouth speaker held up his hand in acknowledgement of his error, though I thought I saw an ironic smile on his lips as he did so.

'I still don't know what it means, though, Henley.' He looked round the tables. 'And I doubt if I'm the only one.'

A man with a glass of wine in one hand and his phone in the other spoke up. '*A privatier is a French word that was used from the 19th century in Germany and some other countries as a title by members of the bourgeoisie*' – sorry, another French word creeping in there – "*and families of substantial financial means in lieu of another professional title. Much like "rentier", it denoted someone who did not have to work to make a living, and who lived off their assets of some size, e.g. interest, profits from investments, et cetera.*' The speaker put the phone down and looked up. 'So only the five foreign words or expressions in that little Wikipedia definition. The Brexiteers won't be happy with that.' He looked at Henley. 'Hope I've cleared things up for people.'

Henley thanked him. He seemed more relaxed now, as if he had removed some obstacles from his path and could proceed unhindered. He gave a small, contrived cough and looked round.

'It was inevitable that, as the year grew older and the seasons turned; as Michaelmas came and went and the days grew shorter,' he continued, 'Gavin's colleagues at the bank would start to ask about the investments from his half of the gold bar, and about his preparations for the journey. And, even though this was never said to his face, if he would set off at all.

'As ever, our protagonist was polite, but evasive in his answers. He had invested the proceeds from the sale of the gold in what today would be called ethical funds. It was an almost unheard of and far more limited field then, as no stigma was attached to oil companies or other environmentally irresponsible firms. People were just waking up to the fact that there was an environment which could be harmed by human hands. But despite the fact that the profits were not so predictable, Gavin did not invest the money in arms manufacturers or heavy industry or banks, preferring to put it into firms that benefited the countryside or local communities in some way. And, even though little was known about the dangers of smoking, he didn't buy any shares in tobacco companies.'

And with a smile, Henley picked up his cigar and drew the rich blue smoke into his lungs.

'I don't understand why he didn't place the money

somewhere more likely to bring him the best return possible,' the Interrupter said. 'His life's at stake and ethical investments aren't exactly a gold mine.'

'Gavin must have had principles,' Henley said drily. 'Which is probably why he accepted the challenge in the first place, and was now preparing to complete his side of the challenge.'

'But it's madness. His one chance is to beat this green man with the investments.'

'Perhaps it's just a story,' the Bulldog said again.

'But Henley's shown us his card.'

'Gentlemen,' Henley interposed. 'The Narrator's watch is ticking. You can argue about this later.'

I had never heard Henley refer to himself as the narrator before, but was relieved to find him alert to the situation that was making me uneasy. I didn't want to find myself caught between Phelbas' intentions, based on a knowledge of wind, weather and water, and the wishes of the guests who didn't want their evening's entertainment curtailed. Despite the fact I too found Henley's tale compelling, and though the boat seemed as securely moored as before, I wondered if the moon was still shining, or if the Phoenician, up on deck, was observing the first signs of the coming storm the forecasts had predicted.

'Though most of you may find Gavin's investment strategy puzzling,' our storyteller continued, 'and he had informed no one, so far as I'm aware, of his plans, he had made arrangements to take two weeks' holiday over Christmas and the New Year.'

'Once again, Henley, I have to ask how you know all

this. Did you work there? Is the bank where Gavin worked our Bank?' It was the Interrupter again, and he was starting to get on my nerves.

'Are you unable to countenance a little willing suspension of disbelief?' the Bulldog said acidly. 'I think the majority of us here would like you to keep your questions to yourself from now on.'

Stung by the remark, the Interrupter turned from his window seat to remonstrate, only to be greeted by a sea of unsympathetic faces and even one or two glares. I was taken aback by the strength of feeling, and then even more astonished by Henley's next remark.

'Storytellers have a sixth sense for these things,' he said, tapping the side of his nose like an actor hamming up his role. 'As our own Narrator knows perfectly well.'

He looked in my direction and I found myself forced to acknowledge the glances of the guests that were turned my way. So I was the one implicated when he had referred to the Narrator's watch ticking a few moments earlier. It was perhaps the oddest thing he had said all evening, and there had been a few. First Phelbas had referred to me as the Captain and now Henley addressed me as the Narrator! I had to presume they both meant I was the one ultimately responsible for the evening. I was the Organiser. Nevertheless, for a moment I felt as if I were losing my bearings. But, refreshed by a draught of beer, that familiar voice resumed, and the world steadied itself.

'If we take a few moments to consider our hero's psychological state during the year since the events I have described, we will find him calm and collected, though barely a minute went by when he was not considering what lay ahead. He had decided in the first weeks of January on a fivefold strategy: he must invest the money from the gold wisely, but according to his principles; he would need to buy and learn how to ride a motorcycle well, because he wanted to match his challenger in every respect; he must locate the Green Chapel; and curiously – at least some of you listening to me in these modern times may consider it curious, like some knight from an Arthurian legend – he swore a vow of chastity.' A few groans accompanied this detail. 'Though it must be said that for Gavin this was not the burden most of you would find it, as he appeared, as yet, immune to the charms of women. The fifth and final side to this strategy of his was that if all else failed, he must be ready to kneel and await the blow of the great axe.'

'Sorry to interrupt,' said a voice that did not belong to the Interrupter, 'but do you have any explanation for this self-inflicted chastity rule, Henley? I mean, I've worked out that your story is set in the late '50s or early '60s, which were hardly Victorian times.'

Henley paused to consider the question, and as I watched his face and saw his gaze turn inwards, it did seem as though he were searching his memory for the answer. The quietness in the saloon deepened. He puffed on his cigar; he had a sip of beer.

'Purity of purpose is strengthened by physical purity,' he said finally. 'At least that's what the ancients thought. Chastity was supposed to be one of the great virtues, and Gavin perhaps thought his cause would prosper if he abstained from any physical intimacy.'

His eyes swept the room, and for the first time must have alighted on the two women listening at the edges of this male enclave. To my surprise, he seemed taken aback.

'Maybe Gavin was turning Buddhist,' Beddoes called out, to a ripple of amusement.

Henley collected himself and turned to the speaker. 'I know many of you will find such an old-fashioned idea hard to accept,' he went on, 'but Gavin must have been an old-fashioned sort of chap.'

He paused, and it seemed the sight of the two women had unsettled him. I couldn't understand why, as Elyssa always joined us after the meal was over. I was growing restless again and wondered how much longer Henley needed to set Gavin on the road to the north, because it was obvious that it would be north he needed to go. But neither Henley, nor Gavin for that matter, appeared ready, and despite this lengthy introduction to the second instalment, no one seemed to be losing interest.

'As a way of keeping this strategy visible before him,' Henley resumed, turning his gaze away from Elyssa and Lovell's cousin, 'the protagonist identified the five sides to his plan in the following manner: Axe, Gold, Chastity, Motorcycle and Chapel. And then, because he felt he needed a symbol to match the stranger's holly leaf with its five points, after days of deliberation, he drew an upright pentagram on a card and inserted in each of its five triangles the initials, A, G, C, M and C. And because he intended the letters to be read clockwise, the A for Axe that stood at the apex of the pentagram was both inception and termination.

'Underneath, and after more consideration, he identified

himself with the word *Quester*, like a character from a medieval romance. For reasons of his own, he was reluctant to name his own profession of banker on the card. He had a small number printed off in a kind of limited edition, which he could never use for business because, like Greneknighte's, his contact details were absent. But it fitted his plan of rivalling the green stranger in every way possible. Nevertheless, whenever Gavin looked at the card – he kept them in his desk at the bank – after the almost mystical thrill had abated, he found himself staring at the empty heart of the pentagram, the pentagon within the pentagon, that contained no letter or token, no image or emblem, and it troubled him that he had found nothing to place there, because it served to remind him of the solitary nature of the quest he had undertaken.'

Henley reached into his pocket and drew out the business card he had flourished earlier as part of his performance. But now I saw how the single card had become two, which he held aloft between the fingers of each hand.

'For those of you wanting to know how I am able to describe his card so precisely, here is another piece of evidence you can examine later.'

I thought he was starting to overdo things, and wished he would get on with the story itself. These conjuror's tricks seemed unworthy of Henley, and I didn't understand why he felt the need for them. His audience, however, unaware of how our time was ticking away, loved it and I heard scattered applause from different corners of the saloon.

'To summarise,' Henley continued, 'the hero has invested the gold, owns a powerful motorcycle he can maintain and ride well; he is as much a virgin as ever, and he has tried to prepare himself psychologically for the blow of the axe by reading obscure self-help books, bought from an esoteric bookshop off the Charing Cross Road. All that remained was to locate his destination, the Green Chapel.

'The weekend before Christmas, he went to stay with his family in the suburban house south of the river where they had always lived. He parked his motorcycle in the garage next to his father's old Rover and gathered together the things he would need. His sister, who was a few years younger than him, brought an old garden chair and sat and watched him in her winter coat as he made his preparations, but she said little, even though she had managed to prise from him something of the nature of his journey. Beyond the walls of the bank where he worked, no one was aware of what had taken place at the previous year's New Year's Eve festivities; almost as though those who were present had sworn a vow of silence to avoid complicity in whatever sequel ensued. His parents remained ignorant of the reasons for their son's desire to go away over Christmas, though they found his purchase of the powerful motorcycle out of character. But though he had been brought up going to church each Sunday and believing in the importance of Christian values, they were liberal-minded enough to assume he knew what he was doing.

'On the longest night of the year, when he was sure even his sister, who seemed to have assigned herself the role of guardian spirit, was sleeping, Gavin wrapped the new bar of gold, which he had bought with the proceeds from his year-long investment, in a cloth and carried it down to the garage, where he placed it at the bottom of one of the motorcycle's saddlebags. He stood and looked at the silent machine that would have to bear his weight on the journey, and wondered if he should check the running of the engine one last time. Taking the silver helmet from where it hung on the handlebars, he placed it on his head and fastened the chin strap. He climbed into the saddle, set the controls, and was about to bring his heel down on the kick-start when he remembered it was past midnight. He sat there for a while, thinking about the madness he had committed himself to and sensing a cold draught around his exposed neck. Then, dismounting, he switched off the light and went to bed.

'Early the following morning, the 22nd December, on the day the earth was turning its face back towards the sun after its moment of hesitation over the Tropic of Capricorn, beneath a grimy sky, the streetlights still glowing amber in the darkness, and with a roar that wakened the neighbours, Gavin spurred the motorbike's engine into life and rode out onto the street. He braked and sat for a moment in the saddle, glad to feel the engine throbbing beneath him, sensing the fuel pulsing through the machine's arteries. With his feet on the ground and his hands holding the handlebar grips, he glanced back towards the house and saw the curtain pulled back from his sister's bedroom window; a white face looked down at him and a hand waved him goodbye. He raised his own gauntleted hand towards her and then, pulling down his visor, he released the clutch, opened the throttle and turned away from his home in the direction of the Great West Road.'

I started, and was on the verge of interrupting Henley myself, so convinced had I been that the only route Gavin could take was north, when I realised I would delay the story's telling further. I glanced at my watch and found that almost no time at all had elapsed since I sat down, yet though Henley seemed to have been speaking again for a while, Gavin was still in London and the fulfilment of his challenge seemed as far away as ever. Instead Henley had filled our ears with details that seemed unnecessary and, recalling the length of the original medieval poem, which I remembered was divided into four parts, or *fitts*, and which I still assumed he was using as his source, I could not imagine how he thought he would reach the end. At some point, about eleven o' clock, presumably with the story still unfinished, Phelbas would expect us to go on deck and I would have to deal with the consequences of the tale's termination. I looked at Henley as he took another drink and wondered why he had decided to tell this story tonight. I glanced round the saloon. All eyes were on him. Everyone was waiting for the storyteller to continue.

'There was no snow or ice, but the wind was spiteful and Gavin was glad to be wearing the leather jacket and trousers, the boots and gauntlets that were part of his equipment. Around his neck he had tied a thick woollen scarf, and he stared at the desultory traffic, the road signs that directed him towards the A40, through the visor of his crash helmet, as though he were indeed a knight from legend embarking on a quest from which there might be no return. But if doubts about what lay ahead made him uneasy, a glance at the bike's crimson fuel tank, with its emblem of a pentangle outlined in silver, seemed to reassure him.

'He crossed the river by Wandsworth Bridge and turned west. He had little company apart from buses, milk floats and early-morning delivery vans, and soon the city fell behind him. In case some of you are wondering, there wasn't as much traffic in those days, and even though the M1 was the sole motorway, Gavin soon found himself passing through High Wycombe and climbing the Chilterns towards Oxford. The motorcycle felt comfortable in his grip, the heat from the engine kept his legs warm, and his misgivings receded as he watched the sun rise in his wing mirrors and saw the wintry light brush the frosty fields with colour.'

'Henley, the make of the bike, please. I'm sure you're keeping it back from us.' I recognised the voice of Dawkins, the motorcycle enthusiast.

'As well as other important details, if I'm not much mistaken.'

It was the storyteller's art, I thought as I heard this last comment – naturally enough, from the Interrupter – what to give and what to withhold. But I didn't say anything.

'Yes, I was waiting for that,' Henley replied, almost with a touch of mischief in his voice. 'Gavin had done his research carefully, and with his family background, even though his position in the bank was relatively minor, he could afford the best. As I've made clear, he wanted to rival his challenger in every way possible, but that did not mean he had to have an identical machine.'

'But he'd bought the best?' Dawkins persisted.

Henley nodded, a smile on his lips. 'He also bought the marque that seemed to suggest a link to the task he had accepted.'

There was a brief pause in which I wondered if those less interested in technical details might grow restless.

'So, it was a Triumph. A Bonneville?'

'Yes.'

'A T120 with a 650cc engine and twin carburettors?'

'I'm not expert enough to comment on the specifications, but that was certainly the model. Gavin sometimes rode it to work and I can remember casting an envious eye in its direction. It was a machine of extraordinary grace and power.'

The sincerity in Henley's voice was unmistakeable. I was beginning to think the old man really had known Gavin, really had run his hand over the leather saddle; had even asked for a ride on the back one September lunchtime, when they had roared helmetless along Lower Thames Street, so close to our point of departure earlier in the evening, while the bells of Magnus Martyr were ringing for Michaelmas; then over Tower Bridge, back through Southwark to London Bridge, and up King William Street towards the looming shadow of the Bank.

And I recalled an earlier version of myself who had also thrilled to that sudden burst of speed, the feeling of weightlessness, of having escaped the chains of gravity; how else had I managed to discover Istanbul and its smoky ferries that I became sidetracked with earlier, but on the back of a motorcycle?

I stared at Henley now in his dark suit that was probably fashionable at the time of his story; tall and dignified, thinning white hair swept back from a broad brow, eyes still bright. He stood by the table and I tried to imagine him as he must have looked over fifty years before: a young man escaping the tedium of the counting house, flying across the river on that wonderful machine.

'By lunchtime, Gavin was in the Midlands,' Henley

resumed, 'the route he had planned unwinding before him towards the destination he was hopeful he had located.'

'How—'

But Henley had his hand raised to pre-empt the question. 'He had a collection of maps in one of the saddlebags, lovely Ordnance Survey ones printed on thick, creamy paper that you could unfold, spread out on the floor and lose yourself among the woods and streams, the winding paths and rippling contours. On these he had marked the places Greneknighte might have meant: three small villages whose names all sounded similar to "Greenchapel", all spelled differently, but all, curiously enough, in the same region. A woman in the post room, whose sister had attended the New Year's Eve dinner, had put him on the track. She had posed the question that no one in the bank dared ask: was he really going to fulfil the terms of the challenge? And when he nodded, she told him he should head for North Wales. "Maybe even as far as Anglesey. That's where he comes from." Gavin had stared at her in surprise, because, like myself, he had found it impossible to detect the green man's origins from his words or manner of speech. "My sister heard it in his voice," the woman said. "As clear as a bell."

'So for five days, Gavin followed this trail, which was not a trail at all, more a rustling he might have heard in the grass. He rode among the mountains of North Wales and down into the narrow valleys with their glum, slate-roofed houses. The weather was damp and drizzly, and each evening, in some draughty guest house or bed and breakfast, he had to try and bring some warmth back into his cold limbs. He pored over his maps in loveless bedrooms and fended off questions from curious landlords and landladies as to why he was travelling at this time of year. And his own questions were returned to him with answers equally unsatisfactory.

'With a racing of his heart to match the motorcycle engine's beat, he found the sites he had identified, but could discover nothing to suggest they had anything to do with his quest: remote clusters of stone houses; three grey chapels with no hint of green or reason to suggest why "green" had ever crept into the villages' names; a watchful dog or two on the doorstep. Disappointed, but still convinced the post-room lady's advice was correct, he crossed the Menai Straits and spent Boxing Day touring Anglesey, but he found there only sheep and the site of the ancient groves where Druids had once prayed; no trace at all of what he was searching for.

'As the brief day began to fade, he returned to the mainland and rode east along the cliffs overlooking the sea. The sun, that never managed to climb far into the sky in these midwinter days, was sinking behind him and cast its pale light over the rocks with their colonies of gulls and gannets. Rows of breakers, foam flying behind them in the wind, crashed onto the stony beaches below as they rolled in from the Irish Sea.

'Gavin came to a halt at the tip of a headland and wheeled the motorcycle off the road. He stood at the edge of the land where it crumbled away into space and stared out over the darkening sea. Part of him felt a sense of relief that he might return home after trying, but failing, to find the Green Chapel, but stronger than this emotion was a sense of frustration at his inability to fulfil the task he had set himself. Deep within him, despite the lack of any directions, he had assumed he would be able to keep the promise he had made. The man's last words, spoken by the severed head he had held in his hand, still sounded in Gavin's ears: *Do not fail me!* it had said, as the blood dripped to the floor.

'With no clear idea of what he was going to do, and feeling the need for some company, a friendly voice in this desolate landscape, Gavin put his helmet back on and started the motorcycle. But although the engine was warm, it took a number of attempts before it was running again and he realised it had misfired a number of times during the course of the day. He had brought some tools with him and was confident he knew how to fix the problem, but he would need light and the day was almost done. He drove back onto the road and at the next signpost turned inland. Pine-covered mountains rose before him in the twilight, but behind them would be a town where he could look at the Triumph, and after something to eat and drink, he would decide what he was going to do in the morning.

'The road wound its way up the mountain. There was no other traffic, and as the light failed completely, flurries of snow gusted out of the invisible sky and it grew colder. The beam of the headlight swept across the ranks of trees as he rounded the curves and, as he slowed the machine to negotiate them, the misfiring grew worse. He needed to stop; he was weary and his arms ached from holding the motorcycle all day. A sense of having made a wrong decision at the junction on the coast filled him, but he could not face retracing his route, and all the while the road continued to climb, uncoiling before him like a fishing line that was reeling him in.

'Abruptly the trees opened out on either side; a rock face reared in front of him and the ground levelled out. He slowed to a halt and the engine faltered and died. Exhaustion seeped through him. He had some food and water, and he had brought a small gas stove, a lamp and a sleeping bag for such an emergency. Changing the plugs might solve the problem with the motorcycle engine, but in this darkness, at this moment, he couldn't face it. He needed to find somewhere out of the wind where he could rest. Taking a torch from one of the saddlebags, he followed a track through a scattering of trees. The wind blew in icy gusts around him and away to his left, through falling snow, he made out a sprinkling of lights from the coast he had left behind. There was the noise of something falling close by, and when he directed the torch beam at the ground, he saw a small bird lying at his feet. He stopped to pick it up and was surprised by its weight, until he realised it was frozen solid, its tiny feet still gripping a twig that had broken off a branch above his head. He shone the torch into the tree and saw other songbirds – finches, tits and robins– like a silent choir, perched lifeless among the leafless branches, frost like age sprinkled over their bowed heads.

'Saddened by this glimpse of the winter's cold, Gavin continued along the path to where it ended outside a small cave, its entrance partly obscured by bushes. It could offer shelter, he thought; it might be possible to light a fire and, wrapped in the sleeping bag, he could even spend the night here until it was light enough for him to fix the Triumph in the morning. The idea of riding through the night in this weather, on a motorcycle with an untrustworthy engine, on a journey that no longer seemed to have a destination, appeared less and less realistic.

'He fetched the motorcycle and parked it beside the entrance, then, shining his torch into the cave, he bent his head and stepped inside. After only a few feet, the narrow walls vanished and Gavin found himself in a chamber whose ceiling rose far above his head. He played the beam of light over the rocks, searching for signs of occupation. He could smell nothing to indicate the presence of animals; he saw no droppings on the floor, and the sounds of the outside world had disappeared. There was the faint sound of water dripping from an unseen source, but otherwise a deep stillness filled the stony room. He scanned the ground for somewhere he could lay his sleeping mat and saw, at the far end where the walls drew together, another low entrance that must lead further into the mountain. Close beside it, at the farthest point from the entrance, there was a pile of leaves. He went closer and bent down to examine it. The bones of small creatures were mixed in with the leaves and dead grass. He wondered what animal used the cave as a lair. A fox, probably, but there was no trace of a dog fox's pungent smell. A female, then? A vixen whose cubs were grown and gone, and who was now alone until the next mating season? Perhaps he could use the leaves and grass to start a fire if he could find some dry pieces of wood among the trees.

'He went back outside, took what he needed from the saddlebags and made a corner of the cave as comfortable as possible. He lit the lamp, and after unrolling his mat and sleeping bag, he heated a can of soup on the gas stove. When he'd finished eating, he brought in an armful of pine branches, which he thought would burn. But as he was about to arrange the wood over the vixen's sleeping place, he was struck by what he was doing. He had already occupied the animal's home; did he want to destroy her bed too? And although a mocking voice told him he was being sentimental, giving animals characteristics they did not possess – how could a wild creature be said to own anything? – he put the matches away and left the branches against the wall. He decided it would not have been a good idea to fill the cave with smoke in any case, as he wriggled down into the sleeping bag and contemplated the night ahead of him.

'Despite his tiredness, it was not easy to get used to sleeping on a thin mat in a vixen's den. Camping was something he had done as a boy scout, and though he folded his towel over a flat stone as a makeshift pillow, he could not get comfortable. Then he remembered the bar of gold, wrapped in its cloth at the bottom of the saddlebag, where anyone could slip their hand inside and take it. For a while, he considered getting up, following the beam of his torch through the entrance tunnel and out into the winter's night, so he could bring the gold inside and sleep with it close beside him. The problem seemed important as he struggled with it in the dark, but in the end, he almost laughed out loud. Like an old miser, he thought, pressing the cold metal against his heart as he slept. He turned on his side, drawing the sleeping bag up around his ears. The ingot and its weight, that was less now than he had hoped for when he originally invested it, could stay outside. If by some twist of fate, it was missing in the morning, his task would have simplified itself. If he did not have the gold, he would be breaking the agreement and would surely be justified in abandoning the mad quest altogether. And if the gold had not disappeared in the night, he would still have no idea where to find the Green Chapel. Had he not done as much as he could to prove himself honourable?

'He lay with his eyes open a little longer, his ears tuning themselves to the displacement of minute crumbs of rock as a small creature ran over them, his nose learning to distinguish between what was animal, vegetable or simply mineral. Without the light of his lamp or the gas stove, the darkness was absolute and he felt its strangeness soaking into him. Like a hermit, a mystic from the past, he lay on his bed inside the mountain, with the inescapable question turning in his mind and the hard stone beneath his head.'

In the saloon, it was equally still. When I glanced at my watch again, I found that the hands had barely moved, as though time itself was slowing; as though we had all stepped into some kind of story time, while the real world continued somewhere else. No one moved or whispered to a neighbour, but as a reminder of where we were, I felt the boat rock beneath us and I heard footsteps on the deck above. Henley took a long drink from his beer glass before continuing.

'That night Gavin dreamed of a figure dressed in black, standing with bent fishing rod, thigh-deep in a turbulent river. The face was concealed from him, like a card from the tarot pack turned face down on the table, and the fisherman's legs were braced against the current. The line tautened as he wrestled with the fish he was reeling in, and even though he was deeply asleep, Gavin could feel a pain in his mouth from where the iron hook had torn his lip. He grew frightened as he was dragged through the churning river towards the figure, because he knew with a dead certainty that once he was caught, he would be slapped upon the block and feel the blow of an axe slicing through his wet, silver-skinned neck.

'Desperate to see the face of whoever had caught him before his head was separated from his body, he found himself out of the water and gasping for breath in the cold air. But as his eyes met those of the fisherman, he realised they did not belong to the green stranger with whom he had an appointment, nor to any man, but were those of a woman whose face was hidden by a scarf, so that only the eyes were visible. However, as her hands tightened around his wriggling body, he felt something brush the back of his neck and woke to find his mouth tasting of blood. Fearing to turn over, he realised that the animal whose home he had occupied had returned. He sensed it sniff his alien presence and heard the pad of velvet feet as it passed by him and left the cave. He waited, motionless, for a few more minutes before he dared to fumble for his torch.

'The chamber was empty, though Gavin could smell the vixen's scent lingering in the air. But now she had found him in her bedroom, he was sure she would not return, and so, despite feeling the cold of the bare mountain beneath him, and having the weight of the strange dream in his head, he slept till a faint patch of light revealed the cave's entrance. Shivering in the early-morning air, he gathered his things and returned to the outer world to find it white and misty with a thin covering of snow on the ground, in which the prints of a fox were visible. The Triumph was standing as he had left it, so after breaking the ice on a nearby pool of water, he washed his face and set about changing the motorcycle's spark plugs. He had brought a few spare parts with him, and as he unscrewed the plugs from their sockets and replaced them with two new ones, he hoped this bit of rudimentary mechanics would work as, feeling cold and hungry, he did not wish to spend the morning with the manual, trying to locate a more serious problem.

'As soon as the Champion plugs were seated, he kick-started the engine and let it run, while he packed everything away. When it had warmed up, he opened the throttle, listening for any sign of the previous day's misfiring, but he could hear nothing irregular. Relieved, he was about to drive back onto the road when a movement among the rocks near the cave's entrance caught his eye. It was the vixen, and, despite the noise, she was watching him. He even had the impression she had been there for a while. She was standing perfectly still, her head turned towards him. Her throat and breast were white, and her russet coat was thick for the winter's cold. He wondered where she had slept, whether she was able to connect the creature in her room with the leather-clad figure before her. He was glad he had not lit a fire in the cave.

'And she stared at him with her amber eyes, smelling the stink of the petrol and exhaust fumes, seeing the blue smoke that drifted away into the trees as he departed. She stared at the tracks the tyres left in the snow, and as the angry sounds faded down the road, but continued to echo across the slopes of the mountain, she turned her back on the man and his machine and re-entered her den.'

I shook my head as the sophistication of the tale Henley was telling increased the longer it went on, though the discovery of a Green Chapel and the meeting with Greneknighte seemed as far away as ever. I did not understand how he could recall so many details, and now he was starting to vary the point of view. From whose perspective did we hear the phrase, 'the man and his machine'? Our omniscient narrator, Henley himself – or possibly even the vixen? I closed my eyes in admiration, pleased to let the wash of words carry me away, as another wave jolted the *Astarte* at its moorings.

The Temptation

As though we were between movements in a piece of music, Henley paused and sat down. A few people left the saloon to stretch their legs, to get some fresh air or relieve themselves. I looked for Phelbas, concerned he might think it was time to cast off, but he did not appear. I thought about asking Henley how much longer he needed, but then decided the question would be churlish, if not downright rude. I might as well tell him to hurry up and get on with it as we all had better things to do, which clearly wasn't the case.

There was little conversation, and none I could hear about the story itself, as though no one wanted to disturb the fragile elements the storyteller had set before us. And then, like the conductor lifting his baton, Henley rose to his feet again and we were back on the motorcycle, gazing down the rocky, tree-lined slopes to where a large country house occupied the middle of an upland vale. It stood in frosty shadow as the sun had not risen over the mountain's shoulder, and was enclosed by a stream. A garden and fields stretched away into the distance. The house seemed old, its stones weathered by wind and rain, and at one corner a tower, complete with crenellations, interrupted its regular features.

'To Gavin,' Henley continued, 'the building gave the curious impression of being larger than it really was, as though a more ancient version, in which there were four towers as well as a moat and drawbridge, had been superseded, but not erased, by the modern house; as if both managed to exist simultaneously. Smoke rose from the chimneys and a number of expensive cars were parked outside.

'Surprised to find such a residence in this remote place, Gavin turned off the road and rode the Triumph up to a pair of open wrought-iron gates. He had decided he would ask his question concerning the whereabouts of a Green Chapel one last time. If the response was a shake of the head, he would return to London, provided the Triumph was up to it, having tried in vain to fulfil the terms of the challenge.

'A sign on a gatepost told him this was *The House*, as if there were no others. Keeping the engine noise to a minimum, Gavin rode along a paved drive and over a wooden bridge. He glanced down and saw a thin layer of ice covered the stream, but that underneath, the water continued to flow. He stared as though through a sheet of clouded glass and saw weeds waving in the current, while fish swam slowly among the green fronds; it appeared as though the underwater world had become their prison for a certain length of time and they were all waiting for the day when they could escape from the spell that bound them.

'He crossed some raked gravel and parked the Triumph near the main door, away from the Bentley and two Jaguars. He wondered if there was a side door he should use, a tradesman's entrance, but while he was hesitating, a man emerged from around the corner of the house. He was wearing a dark suit and a white shirt and appeared to be either some kind of servant or a guest who had not yet gone to bed. He greeted Gavin and asked if he could be of any assistance. Gavin explained what he was searching for, and when the man gave the anticipated response, he thanked him and turned away, resigned – or relieved, he was not sure which – to starting the journey home.

'"There's no need to rush off so quickly, though," said the servant – for that is what he undoubtedly was. "Come inside and have some breakfast." He paused and looked Gavin up and down, as though evaluating his character. "If Bertie is up after all the revelling that went on last night, you could ask him about this Green Chapel. I don't come from round here and he might know something I don't."

'"Bertie?"

'"Lord Bertilak. This is his house. He owns all the land round here."

'So, cheered by the thought of some breakfast, Gavin followed the man through a door, down a passage, and into a warm kitchen. No cook was present, and to his embarrassment, the man made him some breakfast himself, while asking questions about the reasons for Gavin's trip and the powerful motorcycle he rode, all of which Gavin answered as briefly as possible.

'After a while, the man excused himself and Gavin was left to drink his coffee and stretch his legs under the table in peace. A stove was burning in one corner and he could feel the stiffness in his muscles, caused by the many days' riding as well as sleeping in a vixen's cave, start to loosen. But though his body was beginning to relax, his mind kept returning to the task he had not completed, and he found it difficult to understand why Greneknighte had chosen for their second meeting a place so obscure that it could not be found on any map. He had spent a year preparing himself mentally and physically for this challenge, and he found the idea of riding back to London without having faced the man, despite the ordeal he would be spared, deeply disappointing. The pentagram he had drawn in silver on the Triumph's petrol tank and the business cards in his desk at work would always mock him if he failed: Axe, Gold, Chastity, Motorcycle and Chapel; the five words pricked at his conscience.

'There was a noise of footsteps in the passage outside, and the next moment he was no longer alone. A man of middle age, so tall he had to stoop to get through the doorway, stood in the kitchen. He wore tweed trousers and a brown, knitted pullover that hung loosely to his thighs and was stained with what looked like candle wax. On his feet were a pair of leather clogs. Thick, bushy hair covered his head and he appeared to have cut himself shaving.

'"Hello, you must be the man with the Bonnie. Lukas said he'd given you some breakfast." His voice filled the room as he held out his hand. "I'm Bertilak – Bertie if you prefer, and stay around long enough to become familiar."

'Gavin rose and introduced himself, while his host poured himself some coffee. He pulled up a chair and sat down at the table.

'"What brings a city boy like you to this corner of wild and windy Wales?" He burst out laughing at Gavin's surprise. "Of course you're a city boy. No one round here rides a machine like yours. Can't afford it, for one thing. I've already been out to take a peep. And then, no offence, but despite the leather gear, you seem more the sedentary type." He paused to see how Gavin was taking all of this. "Pale skin, educated manners, expensive motorcycle – that can only mean one thing: the city. And probably *the* City, too." His eyes sparkled at the fun he was having. "Almost certainly a banker, but if not, I'd guess something equally disreputable, like insurance." He paused. "I'm not far from the truth, am I?"

'Taken aback by the man's manner, Gavin shook his head.

'"Well, I hope I haven't offended you, but I like playing party games with strangers like you, and we don't get many of them round here." He paused to drink some coffee. "And as I have a bit of an advantage and you may not like childish guessing games, instead of you trying to work out who I am, I'll tell you."

'"I know you're the lord of the manor," Gavin interrupted, unwilling to just sit and be talked to, "and your servant says everything round here belongs to you. So, if you don't mind my asking, and as you already know so much about me, perhaps you could tell me what you do, and then I have something I'd like to ask you."

'A frown crossed Bertilak's face. "I can see I have upset you, young man. I'm sorry. Perhaps I can make amends in some way. Would you like some more to eat or drink?"

'Gavin shook his head.

'"Well, in answer to your first question, I confess I don't have what you would call a job at all, though I do run the estate, which is quite an undertaking. And I'm also master of the Bleheris Hunt. Which is of some significance, as you've arrived just before three days of hunting through the woods and fields round here." He gave Gavin an appraising look. "If you were so inclined, I'd be perfectly happy to let you borrow one of the horses, so you could join us."

'"My riding skills are confined to motorcycles, I'm afraid."

'"A pity. But I have another suggestion, which you might find more agreeable. Lukas told me you were looking for a Green Chapel."

'Gavin nodded.

'"There's a place close by that people who've lived round here a long time call by that name."

'Despite the kitchen's hospitable warmth, Gavin felt a chill creep over his skin. "How far is it?"

'"Three miles at most. A track leading from one of my fields would take you there." Bertilak paused. "If you don't mind my saying, it seems an odd place to have come so far to visit, especially when you didn't even know it was here."

'"I've agreed to meet someone there early on New Year's Day. It's a complicated story; a private arrangement. I'm very grateful for your help."

'A little stunned by what he had heard, Gavin rose to leave, but Bertilak held up his hand to detain him.

'"I need to make amends for my rudeness earlier, and I think I can be of some assistance. Your appointment" – he glanced at his watch – "is four days away. If you would accept my hospitality, I'd like to invite you to stay here until that date, when you can ride over the fields at the crack of dawn, if you wish. The house is full of guests at the moment, who are here for the hunt. My wife doesn't hunt; she detests the very thought of it. While I and the guests are off chasing these savage creatures, I'm certain she would be delighted to have some company, if you are willing."

'Gavin listened in confusion to these suggestions, but Bertilak had not quite finished.

'"I presume your other question concerned this chapel?"

'"Yes."

'He nodded and looked hard at Gavin. "Think it over. I've got some business to attend to, but if you don't have any other plans for the morning and are agreeable, we could meet here for coffee about eleven and you could tell me your decision. In the meantime, feel free to wander round the house and grounds."

'"I could do with a couple of hours to look at the engine on the Triumph. It's been misfiring and I'm not sure I've solved the problem. You haven't got somewhere I could work out of the wind?"

'"We have indeed." Bertilak smiled. "I use a couple of the old stables as a workshop. You'll have plenty of room there. Tools too, if you need them. There's even an electric heater, so your fingers won't freeze when you're trying to adjust some tiny screw. I'd offer to help myself, but, as I said, I'm a bit tied up this morning. I'll get Lukas to show you."

'He rose to his feet and held out his hand. Gavin took it and felt again the strong grasp.

'"Eleven o' clock, then. And I hope you'll decide to stay with us. My wife would certainly appreciate it."

'He left the room as he had entered it, with a little duck of his head, and a few minutes later, Lukas arrived to show Gavin where he could work on the motorcycle.'

I began to realise we were now listening to the third part of the story. At some point, perhaps when Gavin had left the vixen's cave, a page had been turned; the first part could have been titled *The Challenge*, while the second was obviously *The Journey*. And what would this one be called? I wondered once more if all the detail Henley was providing was necessary. And what of the time? What of Phelbas and the weather?

As though to acknowledge my thoughts, Henley turned in my direction.

'No need to worry about the time.' He smiled at me. 'As good narrators know, it can be stretched endlessly, but I will omit the details of how Gavin fixed his engine by cleaning out both carburettors, as it will only be of interest to enthusiasts like Dawkins.'

'Shame,' someone, who might have been Dawkins, called out.

'I will also move the hands of the clock round till the afternoon; until after Gavin decided to accept Lord Bertilak's hospitality, after the light lunch he was able to enjoy in the kitchen, and after his first meeting with the Lady of the house, who showed him to his room, situated in the tower he had seen from the road.'

He turned back to address the saloon in general.

'She was, as representatives of the fair sex almost always are in stories such as this, strikingly beautiful.' He glanced in the direction of Elyssa and Lovell's cousin. 'If I may be so bold, she looked as enchanting as the two ladies we are honoured to have among us tonight.'

And to the embarrassment of both, the old flatterer bowed in their direction. There were a few calls of 'Hear! Hear!' which disconcerted the women further, but I was struck by the look that was exchanged between Henley and the distant cousin; almost as though they were not strangers. But there was no time for me to consider this further, as Henley was anxious to move on.

'She was of slim build with long, chestnut-coloured hair that hung over her shoulders and down her back. Her eyes were green, her skin the colour of milk, and as Gavin lay on the bed, listening to the click of her heels receding down the stone steps of the spiral staircase that led to this secluded chamber, he could not stop himself remembering the way she had walked so gracefully beside him. He had removed his boots and could feel himself sinking into sleep, part of his mind preoccupied with thoughts of the courtesy and kindness she had shown him, but another part struggling to come to terms with the events of the morning.

'Her perfume hung in the air, as he wondered about her striking dissimilarity to her husband: he so rough and seemingly artless, despite his aristocratic breeding; she so delicate and refined; a roe deer in the company of a wild boar. He wondered, too, if he should try to locate his destination before the date of his appointment, the rendezvous with Greneknighte, however one wanted to name it. But, somehow, to arrive sooner than sunrise on the 1st January seemed liked cheating, as if he might be trying to gain an unfair advantage.

'He fell asleep, his mind occupied with the prospect of keeping Lady Bertilak company over the next three days. Above the old four-poster bed on which he lay – the curtains that once enclosed the sleeper were missing – hung a large painting of a hunting scene, complete with panting hounds and hunters on horseback in medieval costume in full pursuit of a sly-looking fox. As he slept and the light that fell through the two windows faded, he heard nothing of the life that went on around him: the crunch of gravel as more guests arrived; the voices of others, dressed in green jackets and boots and carrying weapons of an antique provenance, returned from some excursion; his host, now wearing a hacking coat, and Lukas engaged in conversation on the front steps; the whistle of arrows piercing the wintry air as the Lady, a gaily coloured scarf wrapped about her head to keep out the cold, her body as tautly balanced as the string she pulled, fired them at two targets set up not far from the house.'

'This place sounds like the sort of family home some of us here know quite well,' a junior employee by the name of Jones said, more by way of commentary than active interruption.

And it was doubtless true. I glanced towards the Directors and wondered about their salaries, the wealth they must have accumulated over long years, the country estates they might have acquired, not through inheritance, but simply with the power of cold cash.

'When Gavin awoke,' Henley continued, passing over the remark, 'it was dark, and he could hear dogs barking in the distance. A horse whinnied. For a few moments he was confused and thought it was early morning and the hunt was about to commence, but a glance at his watch told him otherwise. Bertilak wanted to introduce him to the other guests when they had pre-dinner drinks in the library. Gavin had agreed – he could hardly decline the offer, and browsing the library shelves might be a way to pass the time during the next couple of days. However, he had not brought appropriate clothes for such company, and he was not looking forward to the questions he was bound to be asked.

'Realising he needed to get ready, he had a bath and a shave before rummaging through the crumpled clothes in the saddlebag, most of which were not even clean. He found a serviceable pair of trousers and a shirt that was not too creased, but he didn't have a jacket or a tie and the shoes he had been wearing in the evenings looked shabby. He frowned, wondering if he could borrow some things from Bertilak, but they would hardly be the right size. He opened the wardrobe to see if there was a mirror he could comb his hair in, and was surprised to find on the shelves a selection of underwear, socks and shirts; a tweed suit hung from the rail and on the floor were a well-polished pair of brogues; a choice of four ties hung behind the door. A little bemused, he got dressed and discovered that everything fitted him. The jacket was a bit baggy, but perhaps that was how it was meant to be. It was clear, however, that none of the clothes could belong to Lord Bertilak.'

Henley paused to have another drink. He cleared his throat and surveyed us. And I watched his face, trying to imagine how he could have prepared himself for this performance.

'It was after midnight when Gavin rose to leave the table that was littered with the gravy-soaked crusts of bread, the bones and other scraps of the meal they had all enjoyed. He and Bertilak were the only ones left, and he felt relieved he would not have to get up early to take part in the hunt. He wondered what state the other guests would be in, as most of them had drunk more than him. Their confident, strident voices reminded Gavin of the kind of people he worked with, and he suspected they shared a similar profession.'

'What did I tell you?' Jones could not resist adding.

'Throughout the evening, first in the library and later at the dinner table, he had kept the circumstances of his life to himself and, when questioned, offered only vague details about his job in London and the journey he had taken to get here. Out of politeness, he supposed, he had not been pressed further. He had asked about the hunting and was told he had arrived fortuitously as they were all invited for an annual event, a family custom that stretched back to times before the house was built, to the days when the stones of a medieval castle stood on this spot. For three mornings in succession, they would hunt deer, boar and fox as a way of seeing out the old year.

'To all of this Gavin listened with interest, but when they learned he would not be taking part in the hunts, he saw their surprise and felt them staring at him, ready to call him, in the conversations they would have when he was not present, the mystery man, the guest whose presence among them could not be explained.

'But now, they had departed for their beds and only Bertilak remained seated at the table, a selection of Scotch bottles in attendance. His broad face glowed like the embers in the fire.

'"Enjoy your lie-in tomorrow morning, and think of us poor sods riding through the dawn's early light after some fleet-footed deer," he said. He finished his glass and started to refill it. "Don't forget to look after my wife. I've told her she can count on your company."

'Gavin nodded and wished him goodnight. He made his way towards the door, but halfway across the hall, Bertilak called out.

'"Hang on a moment. Let's have a wager to spice up your time here." He paused, and Gavin waited, impatient for his bed in the quiet tower.

'"How about this?" Bertilak said, his eyes on Gavin's face. "What I win in the woods is yours; what you gain while I'm gone you give to me."

'"But what can I win here? It seems a very one-sided bet."

'"I think you'll be surprised by what can happen in the course of a day. And if you gain nothing at all, not even a coin from a game of cards with someone, then you simply say so and the terms will have been fulfilled. I'm sure we can trust each other." There was a pause. "Do you accept?"

'Gavin hesitated, uncertain if he was committing himself to something whose significance he was missing. But after a few seconds he nodded in agreement. This game was trivial in comparison with the test he'd face in three days' time and he did not wish to seem unmannerly.

'Bertilak grinned and strode across the hall to hug him to his chest, as though Gavin were some prodigal son returned.

'"Excellent," he said, and his laugh boomed around them. "I can hardly wait. Sleep well, young fellow."

'Gavin wished him the same and made his way along the passage towards the tower. The wall lamps were dim and their light uncertain, as though it was also past their bedtime, but as he approached the stairs that led up to his chamber, he saw a candlelit figure waiting for him.

'"I thought you might need someone to show you the way up the stairs," the Lady said. "The lights in the tower staircase aren't working at the moment. This is the oldest part of the house and, according to my husband, it will all have to be rewired."

'Gavin followed, embarrassed by this show of hospitality and the knowledge that she had been waiting for him to go to bed. They reached his door, where she stood back while he entered. She was wearing a dressing gown over her nightdress, and a single pearl on a chain lay in the hollow of her throat. The glow from the candle fell on her face, burnishing her red-brown hair.

'"Sleep well," she said. "I wish you sweet dreams, Sir Knight. I look forward to your company in the morning."

She turned, and Gavin watched her shadow grow and shrink over the wall of the tower as she descended the stairs. When she had gone he went into his room and switched on the light. On the white sheets of the turned-down bed lay a pair of folded silk pyjamas.

'I'm glad there's a woman in your story for a change, Mr Henley,' I was startled to hear Elyssa say in one of those pauses when I had the feeling that Henley was turning a page in his head.

'I'm pleased you approve, madam.' Henley bowed towards where the women were seated. 'Though I should warn you that some of the details I still have to narrate might be considered a little… risqué.'

Elyssa's face was lit by a smile. 'You don't need to worry about that,' she said. 'I am what you might call a woman of the world. I've moored with Phelbas in too many strange ports to be easily offended.' She glanced at the young woman beside her. 'And I'm sure my companion feels the same.'

Lovell's cousin nodded in agreement. 'Please don't be concerned on my account, Mr Henley,' she added quietly.

All heads were turned to listen to the women's voices. I could not recall Elyssa ever having commented on one of Henley's stories before, but she was quite right. His previous tales bore no resemblance to the one he was telling now, and had usually presented an ironic view of some aspect of male camaraderie. As a result, they had rarely had space in them for a woman. I watched his eyes resting on Lovell's cousin's face and thought I saw again the flicker of recognition pass between them. It was only momentary, however, for seconds later we were back in Gavin's bedroom.

'Night no longer rubbed itself against Gavin's curtainless windows in his chamber in the tower, and morning was breaking when he was woken by the sounds of voices, footsteps on the gravel, the slamming of doors and car engines being started. Five minutes, perhaps, and it was quiet again and he turned over, hoping to go back to sleep, thankful that he was able to stay here to try and gain some composure before the ordeal on New Year's Day. The dark imaginings of what might transpire seeped into his mind, staining his thoughts and requiring an effort of will to staunch. From outside, in the distance, he seemed to hear the sound of dogs barking, and then there was the noise of his door being opened and closed, followed by a rustling as someone crossed the floor. Alarmed, he opened his eyes and saw a glow of light. A slender figure who could only be Lady Bertilak stood by the window. She placed the candle she had been carrying on the ledge and turned to look at him. Her face was hidden by the hood of her morning gown and he closed his eyes in confusion. Everything in the room was still, and then he felt her sit down on the bed.

'Gavin kept his eyes closed and breathed deeply as he simulated sleep. He had no idea why his host's wife should choose to come to his room as soon as her husband and their guests had left for the hunt. He hoped she would go away, though at the same time her presence so close to him was not unwelcome. Some minutes passed, and he realised he was being foolish. He should stop the game he was playing and discover why she was here.

'He pretended to yawn and opened his eyes. She was looking at him, and he saw she had thrown back the fur-trimmed hood so that her long hair gleamed upon her shoulders; her throat was bare except for the single pearl hanging from a silver chain he had noticed the night before.

'"If the bed-curtains were still here, you might have been safer," she said. "But without them it's not really possible to lie there pretending to be asleep."

'Gavin sat up, protesting that this was not the case, but she laughed and wagged her finger at him.

'"I think we both know the truth of the matter," she said.

'"It would be better if you allowed me to get up and put some clothes on. I feel very uncomfortable talking to you like this."

'"And take off those lovely silk pyjamas I chose myself? Certainly not." She gave him a look, which he found difficult to decipher. "You know we're here all alone. The servants are sound asleep and my husband and his guests will be away for hours, chasing after some poor wild creature. You're my prisoner now, Sir Knight, and I'm not going to give you up so easily."

'Uncertain how seriously she expected him to take this, Gavin switched on the bedside lamp, which lessened the feeling of intimacy she had created in the room.

'"Why do you call me Sir Knight?"

'She laughed again and moved closer to him, so that she was sitting beside his pillow. He glimpsed her pale legs as she made herself comfortable, he saw the vermilion varnish of her manicured fingernails as she folded her hands in her lap.

'"But isn't that what you are? My husband says you've come to meet someone at the Green Chapel on New Year's Day. It seems as though you're involved in some medieval quest. It doesn't sound like the modern world at all."

'Her eyes sparkled, and Gavin found it difficult to meet their gaze.

'"My Lady, I'm sorry to disappoint your romantic ideas, but I work in the City; I drive a Triumph motorcycle. I haven't ridden up from King Arthur's court in Camelot to fight in single combat for the honour of the Round Table."

'"So you say," she answered, "but look around you. Aren't you staying in a castle? Isn't this room a chamber in a tower? And aren't I" – she broke off to give him another disconcerting look – "Lord Bertilak's beautiful wife, who has come to tempt you?"

'But before Gavin could find anything to say in reply, she was on her feet.

'"I do talk so much." She smiled. "You must be wondering what on earth I'm doing in your room so early in the morning." She paused as she looked down at him.

"But you have behaved like a gentleman and I'm sure that will stand you in good stead for whatever task you have to complete in three days' time. I've been remiss, however, in that I failed to greet you as a good hostess should – with a kiss."

'She lowered her head to his and he felt her lips against his cheek. Strands of her hair brushed his face as she stood up again. "Perhaps after breakfast I could show you round the house," she said.

'And then, taking the candle from the windowsill, she crossed the room and was gone. Her slippered feet made no sound on the stone steps as she descended the staircase, and Gavin was left staring at the vacant space she had left behind, as though the air itself had been imprinted with the outline of her body.'

Henley took a drink. A ripple of movement washed through his audience as people shifted their positions or refilled their glasses, but there was no conversation. I avoided looking at my watch.

'Gavin spent the morning in the company of the Lady as she gave him a personal tour of the house, and learned that the hunting party would return in time for lunch. She also told him that it was one of the eccentricities of the three Old Year hunts, as they were called, that only medieval weapons were permitted. Gavin found it hard to imagine. Did they fire their arrows while riding in the saddle like Red Indians from old cowboy films? It seemed far too dangerous.

'At first he felt awkward after her visit to his room, but she made no mention of it and he found her company was more a pleasure than an obligation to his host. No one else seemed to be in the house except for Lukas and a maid, and a small, elderly lady dressed in black, whom they found sitting in front of a log fire in a sitting room and whom his hostess introduced as Morgan. Eyes as sharp as a bird's stared at him from a wrinkled face, and her hand, when he took it in greeting, felt dry and papery. Gavin thought it a strange name for a woman, and when they were alone again, he asked the Lady who she was.

'She looked at him from across the table in the wood-panelled library where they had taken their coffee. The single pearl still hung from its chain around her neck, and though she was dressed for the day in cardigan and skirt, her eyes remained unreadable.

'"If I told you she was my mother, would that surprise you?"

'"Well, yes, I suppose it would," he said, embarrassed by her directness.

'"She had me when she was already in her late forties. But I'm supposed to be a love child, which is rather nice, don't you think?"

'"Of course."

'"My father, who died some years ago, was her second husband and much younger than her." She laughed. "Long ago, in the Welsh village where she grew up, people used to say she was a witch." She looked past Gavin to the bookshelves behind him. "She lives with us now."

'She got up to look at a bookcase. Most of the shelves seemed to be stuffed with books on law and jurisprudence, but she returned with a volume on natural history. He was still puzzling over what she had said, but as she laid the book on the table and opened it, her arm brushed his and he caught a breath of her perfume like a faintly heard yet familiar strain of music. Discomposed by the effect she was having on him, he tried to fix his attention on the pages of beautiful, hand-painted watercolours of birds and animals from the surrounding fields and woods that lay before him.

'For reasons that Gavin could not explain, he and the Lady began speaking ever more quietly as they turned the pages of the old book and gazed at the faded illustrations, which often had accompanying handwritten notes. The room, with its smells of yellowing paper and old time, began to seem like a shell from which the outside world had been sucked away, and inside, where their bodies were cradled, only whispers broke the silence.

'He gazed at a picture of some deer grazing in a meadow. By their lack of antlers, he knew they were does, or hinds as he'd heard them called here, and he recalled being told the previous night that in this first hunt only the females were permitted to be killed. The head of the nearest deer was raised and her ears were tensed as though she had caught some murmur of alarm in a breath of wind that came from beyond the page's edge.

'Both their hands lay upon the open book, and Gavin saw the rubies and emeralds of a gold ring, as Lady Bertilak slowly moved her little finger until it was touching his. A bracelet with a gold charm enclosed her wrist. For a moment he felt the contact, and then she withdrew the hand. His face flushed, and he dared not look towards her.

'And that was where they were when the hunters returned. The house vibrated with the banging of doors, wild shouts and unrestrained laughter, and Bertilak's huge voice boomed down the passageways and echoed from the stone walls as he stamped up the stairs to find them. The door was flung open and there he stood, filling the doorway, the carcase of a young deer draped around his shoulders.

"'Well,' he said, his voice gusting through the bookshelves, "what have you two been up to, while we've been out shedding blood?"'

Henley looked around, and I had the eerie sensation that the question was also addressed to us. He was using different voices for each character in the story, and Lord Bertilak's reverberating tones were particularly effective. If the question was meant to be provocative, however, no one responded, and we found ourselves swept onwards to the evening, as Henley slipped back into his narrator's voice.

'When it was dark and owls were calling from the woods outside, in the hall where Gavin had agreed to exchange his winnings, they feasted on venison while logs burned in the hearth, and he wondered what he could give Bertilak, for it seemed feeble to have nothing to offer in return. There were more guests than there had been the previous evening, and Gavin did not know if they were staying in the house or if they had just been part of the hunt. He sat opposite Bertilak at one of the oak tables and ate and drank with the others, joining in the conversations when needed, but preferring to observe all that was going on around him. He was not a great meat eater, but had never tasted anything as succulent as the thin slices of pink venison that were served on plates piled with vegetables. Lady Bertilak sat beside her husband, but though their glances met from time to time, as soon as the meal was over, she rose to depart with some of the other women, leaving the hall dominated by the voices of men.

'Gavin watched her leave, but when he returned his gaze to the table, he found Bertilak's eyes upon him. His host smiled broadly.

'"Well, if I'm not much mistaken, we have an agreement to exchange the day's winnings, and I think now is as good a time as any."

He got to his feet and banged a glass down on the table until the conversations ceased.

'"I hope the food you've been eating has been to your satisfaction," he began, his voice resounding around the great room. "As most of you know, we're fortunate to have an excellent chef here in the house. And the meat you provided yourselves, so you've only got yourselves to blame if you didn't enjoy it."

'Cries of approval greeted his words.'

'All this talk of fine food is making me hungry again, Henley. It sounds better than what we've had on the boat.'

A few voices echoed this speaker's comment – much to my annoyance, as I was responsible for organising the catering – but Henley chose to ignore them, taking the opportunity to have a drink and examine his dead cigar resting in the ashtray.

'A lot of wining and dining in this story of mine,' he said absently. 'A lot of people sitting listening to someone talking…' he paused, 'at great length.' He looked round at us, pressed into the saloon's confines. 'I hope I'm not keeping anyone up beyond their bedtime, but if I'm truthful, I'm afraid there's a bit of a way to go before we reach the end of all this.'

He glanced in my direction with what I took to be a wry smile. I nodded. We both knew that things would run their course now. Henley's tale would reach its conclusion in its own good time, which was what his audience wanted. What concerned me was how Phelbas would react when the deadline he had set was reached. I looked at my watch and saw it was ten to eleven. Our Phoenician sea captain remained on deck.

'Once he had everyone's attention, Lord Bertilak described in gory detail the morning's hunt,' Henley continued. 'I will spare you most of this, not just because we have ladies among us, but because the descriptions seem to me more symbolic than narrative.'

I listened as Henley critically analysed his material, but there was no time to reflect on his comments.

'"In the frosty fields, before they had a chance to escape into the woods," Lord Bertilak said, "we shot four does, the hum of our arrows barely breaking the morning's stillness. Then we gutted them on the spot, threw the innards to the hounds, and after tying the carcasses to poles, left them to be brought back to the house. It was a fair piece of work, accomplished while one of our number was dreaming in the warmth of his bed." He grinned at Gavin. "But why shouldn't he? He didn't come here to hunt, but for reasons of his own." He stopped and appeared to say something no one heard. Gavin gazed at the empty seat beside his host and thought of his early-morning visitor, as Bertilak left the hall, returning moments later with Lukas, who was helping to carry one of the deer they had hunted. The two men stopped where everyone could see them.

'"Collect your winnings, young fellow. This is the deer I

killed myself, which I give to you as my side of the bargain we made last night."

'Bertilak and Lukas let the body slide to the floor and Gavin, to his embarrassment, found himself being beckoned to join them. Each head was turned to watch him. The dead animal lay on the stone floor, disembowelled, though still unskinned, its delicate neck limp, its eyes vacant, two arrows protruding from its bloodstained flank. Bertilak placed a broad arm around his shoulders and looked into his face. There was a sense of expectation in the hall, and Gavin could feel his host's guests, these strangers, probing at his heart, searching for an explanation for his presence among them.

'"And what have you to offer in return?" the great voice asked.

'Only then, exposed and on his own, did Gavin find his answer. He reached up and brushed his lips against Bertilak's rough cheek.

'"A kiss. That was all I managed to win today."

'Something that might be called a sigh ran round the hall as the guests puzzled over the gesture. His host looked at him with a smile on his face.

'"I see," he said. "A very small thing in comparison. I wonder how much blood and toil it cost to win." He raised a hand to forestall any objections. "But, of course, that's not the point. However, I would be interested to know how you gained your winnings. You have heard a full report of how I came by mine, while you, I presume, lay sleeping."

'Feeling more confident, less of an outsider now that his gift had been accepted, Gavin smiled in turn. "I'm grateful for your account," he said. "I enjoyed listening to the details of your exploits so early in the morning when, as you say, I was still in bed. But you provided these voluntarily, for the benefit of your guests here. How I gained the kiss I have given you is my affair and outside the terms of our agreement."

'Perhaps he was surprised by the reply, but Lord Bertilak did not show it,' Henley commented. 'He gave Gavin a comradely embrace and they reaffirmed the terms of their bargain for the following day. People began to drift away to bed, and after a conversation about the hunt he would be missing in the morning, Gavin found himself retracing his steps along the corridor to the tower. And in the dim light he found, as on the previous night, the Lady waiting for him.

'She gave him a smile of greeting, but not a word was spoken between them. He followed her up the stairs in the candle's shifting light and heard the rustle of her nightgown over the stone steps. They reached the chamber, and she stood back as he opened the door. All was as before. And after she had left him, he stood between the cold walls and saw the silk pyjamas folded upon the sheets and realised she had been here while he was still in the hall. He unfolded them and thought of how her hands had touched the material such a short time ago; he inhaled the air, trying to draw what remained of her scent into his lungs. He gazed round the room for some other sign of her presence, but could find nothing.

'Later he lay between the sheets, remembering the way she had teased him that morning. Had she been flirting with him to see how he would react? Or was he imagining things?

Was she not simply a very attentive hostess? His eyes fell on the key resting in the door lock and he knew he could turn it if he wished; he felt certain she would slip into his room as soon as her husband and the guests had left for the morning's hunt. It was as if he had become part of a ritual he could not escape and whose purpose he did not understand. In the quiet of the night, in this chamber in a tower, he thought he could hear his heart beating. He looked again at the door with its medieval key, from which a leather tag hung, but he did not get up to turn it. He lay deliberating over this failure of his a while longer and then he turned out the light.'

I liked the poetic style Henley was able to slip into in these introspective moments and I enjoyed the psychological insights he was providing into Gavin's actions, but I could not get over his ability to master so much material. I wondered if I was alone in noticing these things, and I found myself looking at Lovell's cousin. The expression of surprise on the storyteller's face when he had noticed her for the first time suggested she was not unknown to him. What did she think of Henley's story?

'Through the fog of his sleep, as day was breaking,' Henley continued, 'Gavin heard car doors banging, engines firing into life, gravel sliding beneath the wheels as the hunters departed, and he recalled what Bertilak had told him: how the second hunt would be for boar, though, as with the other traditional hunts, only arrows fired from a conventional bow or a crossbow were allowed. However, once the animal was cornered and the battle was no longer being fought on horseback, spears were permitted. Gavin had never heard of anything like it, and he wondered if the women guests took part. A woman had brought down one of the deer the previous morning, he had learned, so it did not seem out of the question. In the distance the hounds begin to bark, and, in the same moment, he felt the vibration of his door opening, the darkness lightening as a candle was brought into the chamber, and he heard the Lady's footfall as she crossed the room to sit on his bed.

'He opened his eyes and saw she carried a two-branched candlestick, which she placed upon the window ledge. He switched on the lamp and found she had not come in disguise this morning, for the hood of her gown was thrown back. She smiled.

'"Would you mind if I took this off?" she asked. "It doesn't feel cold in here."

'Before he could reply, before he had the chance to comment on the unlikelihood of her claim, she was laying her gown at the foot of his bed. Her russet hair hung down her back and over her white lace nightdress. He saw the single pearl at her throat, the gold bracelet, the ruby-and-emerald ring, and he was aware that her pale skin was visible through the garment's lacy material. He tried to find somewhere else for his eyes to look as her body, so thinly covered, rested so close beside him. He felt his cheeks reddening as he realised the effect she was having on him, and knew it was impossible for him to get up and escape the situation.

'The Lady leaned across and kissed Gavin once, lightly, on the mouth. "You see, I have remembered my manners this morning," she said. "And I have a question for you." She looked at him gravely. "How much love should a hostess show an honoured guest?"

'"How much *love*?" Gavin was alarmed, but the Lady smiled in the winning way she had.

'"Yes, love," she repeated. "It's an old word and has many meanings, but I think we both know what I mean."

'"Do you make a distinction between male and female guests?" he asked, realising not only that he had no choice but to play this game of hers, but also how dangerous it might be for him.

'She smiled. "Perhaps."

'"But why do you ask me? I think you overestimate my experience in such matters. I am flattered by all your kind, loving attentions, but maybe I am not the man you think I am."

'Beneath the sheets, however, the man knew his body told a different story. He thought she was looking, with little sign of ambiguity, at the empty space in the bed beside him, and he felt himself weaken. But he could not suggest such a thing, and what if he was misunderstanding what he took to be her signals – what then? What about his duties to the man who was her husband? What of his vow of chastity?

'She gave a sudden, involuntary shiver, and Gavin could see she was colder than she had claimed. There were goosebumps on her arms and, though he tried not to, he could not help noticing how her breasts pressed against the material of her nightgown.'

Henley paused, as though he expected some ribald interruption at this point, but none came. He glanced at the two women, as it seemed these details were embarrassing him, but when he saw they were unshocked and remained as absorbed as everyone else, he took a drink and returned to the chamber in the tower, which none of us had left.

'There was a silence, as if each of them was unwilling to speak. As though they both knew the next move, but were reluctant to make it. At last she looked him in the face.

'"You do not seem such a gentleman this morning, Sir Knight."

'Gavin looked away from her towards the window, relieved she had chosen to break the spell.

'"I'm sorry," he said. "My appointment on New Year's Day is on my mind. Forgive me if I've been remiss."

'She nodded. "Perhaps I can help you." She looked at him. "I'll give the matter some thought and then, tomorrow, if we have another encounter like this, I might be able to set your mind at ease." She smiled. "Who knows?"

'She got to her feet and put on the morning gown, then, bending over him once more, she placed her hand behind his head and drew his face towards hers, kissing him a second time, her lips lingering on his, so he could feel their softness.

'"If you like, I can be your guide again after breakfast," she said, as she took the candlestick and left his side.'

'Well, Henley, you've never told a story like this before,' the Interrupter said, and I heard murmurs of agreement. But Henley, apparently anxious to keep his story under full sail, swept on.

'Dressed warmly for the outdoors, the Lady came to find him as he sat talking to Lukas in the kitchen.

'"Today, I'll show you the grounds, including the gardens and stables," she said. "And then, if you wish, we can have coffee in the library, like yesterday."

'Gavin was pleased with these arrangements, particularly as they meant he would be able to spend some time in her company without feeling so powerless, so exposed beneath the sheets in his silk pyjamas, while she sat so close to him.

'"We'll take Lancelot and Guinevere," she said, as he followed her through the house. "I'm sure they'd love to meet you."

'And the two Labradors, one the colour of cream, the other a glossy black, wagged their tails, as good-natured dogs do, and accompanied them on their tour – though which of the two was the knight and which his lover, Gavin could not later recall.

'"Labradors are not hunting dogs," the Lady said pointedly, as they walked across the fields, where the grass was damp with dew.

'The sun was a colourless disc in the empty sky, and a cold wind blew in their faces. Gavin wore his scarf and leather jacket and felt scruffy beside her, a peasant the lady of the house had taken a fancy to, as in some old folk song; songs which tended to end badly for all concerned, he seemed to remember. But out here in the public domain, far from the intimacy of his bedroom, she was Lady Bertilak – friendly, polite and perfectly mannered, as though there never had been a conversation about how a good hostess should behave, as though she had not taken off her morning gown so he could glimpse her pale skin through her nightdress's thin material, as though he had not caught her gazing at the unoccupied space in the bed beside him.

'They each took a dog as they followed a path that skirted

the house, and though Gavin chatted away amiably enough, as soon as he glimpsed the track that led in the direction he must take in two days' time, he became preoccupied. He stared at the wooded slopes that rose above the pastures, but saw no sign of a building.

'She saw him looking to where the chapel must lie, and squeezed his arm.

'"Don't think about it now," she said. "There's no point. But, as I said, if you don't decide to lock your door tonight, I can offer some advice you might find helpful for this quest of yours."

'She said no more, and Gavin did not ask. He didn't wish to muddy the distinction between the two worlds they had created for themselves, or rather, she had created.

'They walked back to the house, and she went to find Lukas so he could bring them coffee in the library. Gavin climbed the stairs and sat in the same chair as the day before. The natural history book with its delicate illustrations lay open on the table, and he leafed through the pages until he found what he was looking for. She joined him soon after, and then Lukas arrived with the coffee. Once he had gone they sat there, side by side, and amidst the quietness of the books, Gavin felt the intimacy of their early-morning encounters returning.

'"That's who they're hunting this morning?" he asked, indicating a painting of a wild boar rooting through the undergrowth beneath the branches of an oak tree. In the foreground, clusters of green and gold acorns lay, yet to be discovered.

'But before the Lady could reply, they heard the noise of

cars returning, voices calling and doors slamming, the sound of dirty boots on the stone stairs and then, far quicker than seemed possible, as though he had returned, in stealth, early from the hunt and had been waiting in the wings of a stage to surprise them, Bertilak threw open the library door and stood looking in. With him came the smells of earth and rotted leaves, of black, slippery mud. His clothes were wet, a red gash showed through a rip in his corduroy trousers, and in his arms he carried a boar's head, from whose neck blood still dripped.

'The Lady gave a cry and was on her feet, glaring at her husband. "This is too much, Bertie! You know my feelings about hunting."

'"I know. I'm sorry. But I couldn't wait to show our guest what I, we, have been doing all morning; the war this monstrous creature has waged against us."

'"The only monstrous creature I can see is you – and your friends. You're the ones waging war, invading the places where these animals live." She turned to Gavin. "I apologise, you'll have to excuse me. I expect we'll see each other later."

'She crossed to the door, forcing her husband to step aside to let her out. He stood there a little ruefully now, the weight of the animal's head making his arms sag.

'"She's right, of course," he said. "I regret the interruption, but you missed something this morning, young fellow."

'And Gavin stared at the severed head his host had brought to show him: the savage tusks, the empty eyes, the tongue lolling between lifeless lips.'

There was a pause. The boat rocked against the quay, as a wave washed against it.

'These hunts,' someone who was not the Interrupter

said, 'I mean, I've been hunting, I know what it's like, and I've never heard of one where they use bows and arrows or spears. It would be incredibly dangerous—'

'And illegal,' the real Interrupter could not resist adding.

'It seems so far-fetched, Henley.'

'Almost as far-fetched as challenging someone to a beheading game,' the Bulldog said.

I noted the irony in his voice and wondered if the other two had heard it, or were their worlds too literal for such subtleties? The Interrupter, however, was back in the chase.

'Exactly,' he said. 'As I've been saying all evening, and with no disrespect to Henley, the story is just not believable.'

This was getting tiresome, and I thought of how our time was being wasted in a discussion that led nowhere. I waited for the Bulldog to come to Henley's aid, but to my surprise, he was not needed.

'I said earlier that the story I am telling this evening is true,' Henley said, putting the glass he had been drinking from back on the table. 'I can't compel you to believe me, but you might do me the courtesy of taking my word when I tell you I witnessed the events at the bank's New Year's Eve dinner.'

'But what about now?' the Interrupter continued. 'You weren't with this Gavin in North Wales, in Lord Bertilak's castle, or whatever it is. You weren't in the bedroom or the library to overhear these conversations. How can this be anything other than something you've invented?'

'For goodness' sake!' I said in annoyance, anxious to forestall a fruitless debate about Henley's sources. I rose to my feet, but the Bulldog was there before me.

'Gentlemen, and ladies, I think we must allow Mr Henley to proceed with his story,' he said in that authoritative voice of his. 'Without any further interruptions.'

Some voices called out in support, and Henley nodded his thanks. The Bulldog and I sat back down. Talking ceased. The tale continued, though the Interrupter looked frustrated by his lack of support. And Phelbas was nowhere to be seen.

'To Gavin's regret, the Lady did not appear at dinner,' Henley went on, as if there had been no disruption at all; as if he had simply turned the page. 'He wondered if she and his host had quarrelled, but the evening followed the same pattern as before: conversation with the other guests, attempts to deflect questions that were more challenging this time, and a meal of roasted wild boar, obviously.

'"With fresh truffles!" a guest sitting near Gavin exclaimed, sniffing the plate in front of him.

'When the eating was done, Bertilak got to his feet and, after banging his glass upon the table for silence, recounted the events of the morning. As with the first hunt, I will omit the more unpleasant details,' Henley put in, 'though the final struggle between Lord Bertilak and the giant boar is significant, so, ladies, and anyone with a squeamish stomach, my apologies in advance.

'Like the other guests, Gavin listened as Bertilak described how they had flushed out the boar, firing arrows that just skimmed off his crusty hide; how he had caused some of the horses to rear with his short, aggressive charges, and how he had savaged the hounds, driving them off, whimpering, to lick their wounds. Finally, they had forced the tired beast into a stream, from whose steep banks no escape was possible. Leaving his horse, Bertilak had plunged into the shallow water and confronted the creature.

'"There was blood on his tusks and murder in his eye," Bertilak's voice boomed through the hall, commencing to mime the fatal struggle. "There was nowhere else for him to go, so like the brave brute he was, he turned to face me, bristles raised, a snarling grin on his foaming chops. But I had my ancestors' sword, and as we grappled, man and beast, in the icy stream, that was what I dug deep into his wicked heart."

'He stared round the hall, as if daring anyone to deny this extravagant account of what had happened. Gavin sat still, knowing his moment was approaching, but realising also that his host's self-aggrandisement – he couldn't find another word to describe it – was starting to irritate him.

'"It took four of us to drag him out of the water and up the bank, where we gutted him and gave the yelping dogs their reward. Then we tied the carcase to two stout poles and brought him home."

'He called out for Lukas and the servant appeared, struggling to carry the boar's head on an enormous platter. Bertilak took it from him and looked at Gavin.

'"Come and collect your winnings. This, by rights, is yours."

'He held the head, with its long snout and smile that now seemed ironic, out towards Gavin, who, rising to his feet, stepped away from the tables. He had drunk more wine than he had intended, and moved with caution. He did not wish to make a fool of himself in front of the watching guests, who he suspected would like nothing better. And despite Bertilak's generous hospitality, he sensed a rivalry in the man's spirit he found hard to contain.

'"Yesterday, a young deer; today a ferocious tusker. Here, take it. It's yours," his host said, when Gavin stood before him.

'But despite the wine, Gavin was not about to reach out and accept the platter. He had seen Lukas struggling to carry it and knew he would do no better. He gave Bertilak what he hoped was a gracious smile.

'"I'm very honoured," he said, "but I couldn't possibly carry such a weight. As you know, I'm not used to this outdoor life of yours, these fights to the death with wild creatures, who I'm sure are not as wicked as you suggest." He looked at Bertilak. "He did taste delicious, however."

'"As you wish." And Bertilak passed the platter back to Lukas, while Gavin waited for the chance to present what he had won, for it seemed only courteous that Bertilak should ask him, as part of the ceremony that this exchange had become.

'"I hope you also had some success?"

'Gavin nodded and, stepping forward, he placed a kiss on the other man's cheek.

'"The same as yesterday?"

'"Not quite. Although my winnings, as you call them, cannot compare with yours, I felt more confident today. Not quite the novice I was."

'A smile gathered at the corners of Bertilak's lips. "And what did you win as a result of this increased confidence?"

'They were standing close together in the space beyond the tables. Lukas had returned to the kitchen, bearing the boar's head, and though every eye was fixed upon them,

Gavin sensed the intimacy of the moment as he reached up to place his arm around his host's neck, before kissing him on the mouth. He had rehearsed the action in his mind during the afternoon, but was still shocked by the contact with the other man's lips.'

'A bit daring for the early '60s,' Beddoes said. 'Couldn't you be arrested for that sort of thing back then?'

'Quite possibly,' Henley answered, 'but I assure you, that is what happened. The detail is important to the story.'

Voices of support reassured him. Most of the listeners were two generations younger than Henley, but I was struck once again by how much the telling of this tale meant to the old man. He didn't just want us to be entertained, but to understand his story. I saw his glance stray towards Lovell's cousin and the impression began to grow in me that she had become the most important member of his audience.

'The two men stood looking at each other, their faces only a few feet apart,' Henley resumed. 'Gavin felt in need of another drink, but Lord Bertilak did not appear discomfited by what had happened, though a hush had settled over the other guests.

'"I know that how you earned these winnings is your own affair," Bertilak smiled, "though, as you must realise by now, I enjoy describing the blood and guts of my own hunting. Tomorrow will be your last day with us. I'll be up early chasing some wily fox, while you're still sleeping. I wish you good fortune and look forward to discovering how successful you've been tomorrow evening."'

Henley sipped at his beer and I wondered if he would

not be more comfortable sitting down. He had been standing for what seemed like hours, though time aboard the *Astarte* appeared to have slowed almost to a standstill. I asked myself how much longer the Phoenician's patience would last.

'When Gavin left the dining hall,' Henley resumed, 'he found himself hoping the Lady would be there to escort him to bed as on the previous two evenings. She did not disappoint him. At the foot of the stairs that led to his chamber, a lighted candle in her hand, he saw her waiting, though the small flame would not stay in the same place as he approached, and he regretted the amount of wine he had drunk.

'"I thought you might need something to light your way to bed," she said, as she had said before, and turned to climb the stairs. The candle glimmered as he followed her, and he found the winding steps difficult to negotiate. She was standing outside his door when he reached the top, and he put his hand on the wall to stop the tower swaying. He thought he heard her giggle.

'"Well, Sir Knight, I suspect you'll be very bad-tempered in the morning, if I chance to pass this way."

'Gavin took his hand off the wall and tried to stand straight. "I'll be fine," he said. "Please tell me when you'll be coming, so I can get up in advance to greet you properly."

'"You know I can't do that. You want to make it sound like an assignation, and that would never do. You know, however tiresome my husband may be, I'm still a married woman. Anyway, we talked about all that this morning."

'He found it difficult to remember such a conversation,

and the little he did recall seemed to have been inconclusive. The scent of her was clouding his senses, and he leaned forwards, wanting to place his lips at its source in the curve of her throat. He felt his balance going and had to hold on to her waist to steady himself.

"'Sir Knight, I think I had better put you to bed, though I'm not sure that falls within the duties of a good hostess. I don't want you doing something you will regret."

'She eased his head from her shoulder and opened the door. He followed her into the dark room, but found he had to sit down on the bed. She placed her candle on the window ledge and did not switch on the light. Then she was standing in front of him, helping him out of the tweed jacket. His tie and shirt followed. She bent down to untie his shoes and he kicked them off, pulling off his socks at the same time.

"'You'll have to stand up for the last bit," she said.

"'It's all right, I can manage," he replied, realising what she intended, but she pushed his fumbling hands away and unzipped his trousers. He climbed out of them, and wondered light-headedly where all this was leading, but was forced to sit back down. He tried to focus on her face, the expression she wore in the shadowy light, but stepping away from him, she blew out the candle and spilled the night back into the room. Some moonlight slipped through the glass, so he could see her standing beside the window. He wished his head was clear; he wished he could master his limbs better. He wished he could see inside her thoughts. She took a couple of steps and drew him to his feet again. The air was full of her quicksilver movements, and he felt clumsy and earthbound in comparison. He wanted to draw her against him, to kiss her as she had kissed him that morning.

"'I'm sure you don't want to sleep in these," she said, as she pulled his underpants down his legs in the darkness.

'He stood there before her and struggled to maintain his balance, to stand erect, because he felt sure if he sat down again she would be gone, but into his head came a picture of the Triumph's fuel tank and the silver pentagram he had inscribed there. He thought of the five letters and their importance for him. On his limited-edition business card he had identified himself as a quester, but the goal of his quest seemed hidden by a mist, in which he had lost his way.

"'Sleep well, Sir Knight," he heard her say as she crossed the room and closed the door behind her.

'Gavin sat back down on the edge of the bed, trying to drive out the effects of the alcohol he had consumed. He heard a match being struck on the landing and presumed she had relit her candle to descend the stairs. He tried to find his pyjamas, but was unable to locate them.'

As Henley paused at what seemed to be another break in the narrative, I glanced across at Elyssa and Lovell's cousin. I had no doubt the Phoenician's wife was a woman of the world, as she had claimed, but what of her young companion? What was her background? Was she an outsider, as we insiders called those who did not work at the Bank? She might well be shocked, in this room full of men, by some of the details of the story she was listening to, and I was surprised by Henley's nerve. His manners were so old-school, yet here he was describing a near seduction scene in intimate detail in the hearing of a young woman whose presence seemed to mean something special to him. And I did not understand why.

'Night no longer rubbed itself against Gavin's curtainless windows in his chamber in the tower, and morning was breaking when he was woken from a bottomless sleep.'

I started. Henley was continuing his tale, but he had used exactly the same image before; indeed the entire sentence struck me as familiar. And I thought there had been other repetitions in this third section I had taken the liberty of calling *The Temptation*, as though he'd been having lessons in the devices of oral narration from some blind poet like Homer. And why not? For all I knew, the man was a classical scholar, familiar with such techniques. The architecture of the story he seemed far from finishing was now so immense, so carefully constructed, it was inconceivable he had not prepared himself for this evening in as many ways as possible.

'Gavin must have slept through the sounds of the hunters' departure, but the click of his door opening and the sound of the key turning in the lock dragged him into wakefulness. He opened his eyes as the candlelit figure of Lady Bertilak crossed the floor and repeated her actions of the previous two mornings, though today she carried a three-branched candelabra, and, as Gavin recalled the events of the night before, confirmed by the realisation that he lay naked beneath the sheets, he groaned to himself. He had wanted to be dressed and armoured against her subtle, and not-so-subtle, advances on this last morning, but instead, in his drunkenness, he had permitted her to undress him. Furthermore, she would know he was without pyjamas, because she had probably taken them away herself. Though his head was clear and pain-free, he could not prevent another sigh from escaping into the room.

'"What, sighing again?" she said. "And after all I've done for you. That really is too bad, Sir Knight. But here is the good-morning kiss I always give you in my role as a loving hostess."

'She bent down and brushed her lips against his cheek and, glimpsing an expanse of her white neck, he guessed that beneath the morning gown, she too was naked. He felt weak at the realisation as she sat down beside him, but when he stretched out his arm to switch on the bedside lamp, she laid her hand on his to prevent him.

'"Don't you think we have enough light to see each other by?" she asked softly. "This is your last morning beneath my roof, the last time I shall be able to slip into your room when the rest of the house is either sleeping or riding with my husband on their wild pursuit. And as it is the last time we have the opportunity to be alone like this, I have locked the door so we cannot be disturbed." She leaned closer. "So now, Sir Knight, you really are my prisoner."

'And she took the key out of her gown's pocket and held it up for him to see. On an impulse, Gavin tried to grab it from her. The Lady laughed, clinging fiercely to the medieval key, and as they wrestled on the bed, her gown slipped open. They stopped struggling and looked at each other. Both were breathing rapidly, and her cheeks were flushed. She made no move to close her gown, as she stared at his naked chest.

'"Whatever happened to your silk pyjamas?"

'"The maid who tidies the room must have moved them."'

Henley paused and looked at Elyssa and Lovell's cousin. 'I hope I haven't overstepped the bounds of modesty in my description of this scene,' he said.

'If the details are important to the story, then you must describe them to us, however immodest,' the younger woman reassured him.

'You are always a perfect gentleman, Mr Henley, in your concern for us,' Elyssa added. 'I can't imagine you would ever offend us. However, I'm not sure I'd like to have Lady Bertilak as a friend. She seems such an artful woman.'

Henley nodded and said something to her I didn't catch, before looking round the saloon. 'Apologies, gentlemen, but I need a breather for a few minutes.'

'You can't stop here, Henley, for God's sake,' the Interrupter said.

'I think you'll find he has,' I heard the Bulldog answer.

Henley sat down and lit another cigar. He must be exhausted by the performance, I thought, and was pleased to observe that his neighbours were not talking to him, but giving him a chance to have a break. I had made up my mind not to look at my watch, and to wait until Phelbas appeared to tell me our time had run out. Like everyone else, I was frustrated by the interruption and could not help wondering if Henley had deliberately halted the tale at this point.

In a few minutes, however, he rose to his feet with a freshly lit cigar in his hand and the whispering ceased.

'This chamber in the tower where Gavin had already spent three nights was not large, though the ceiling was high, and the air, scented as it was by the Lady's presence, smelt of old stone; stone that had been cut, chiselled and mortared, and endured through many centuries. In this space, on the bed in which Gavin had slept, they could sense each other's desire, how very close their bodies were. And then, perhaps because he had failed to embrace her, as she might have been expecting, before he could stop her, Lady Bertilak slipped under the covers beside him.

'"You don't mind, do you?" she whispered. "It's not so warm out there." She touched his lips with hers. Her head lay on the same pillow as his, and he realised they were lying there like lovers.'

'Henley, this is beginning to get very racy indeed,' someone said quietly. 'You seem very concerned about whether it's suitable for the ladies, but what about chaps like us?'

There was some laughter.

'This isn't the moment to start discussing the tastes of chaps like you,' Henley answered drily, and returned us to the Lady and her next words to Gavin.

'"That's your second good-morning kiss, Sir Knight, another chaste one, and if you're thinking that I'm going beyond what is permitted in our circumstances, please remember that I am more or less respectably dressed, and you aren't." And she covered her mouth with one hand, her eyes shining with the laughter that overcame her.

'Gavin tried to remain calm, but when she placed one hand on his chest, he protested. She apologised and, seeming to notice for the first time how her gown had come open, she drew it together. Her other hand, however, remained where it was. For a few moments neither of them spoke, as Gavin struggled to master himself.

'"You are very cold this morning, Sir Knight. Not like you were last night, outside on the landing."

'"I shouldn't have drunk so much."

'"Please don't pretend it was only the wine." She stared at him, and her eyes seemed to glitter, rather than sparkle. "Why is it so hard to return the love I offer you? Is it because there is someone else who holds your heart?"

'"There is no one," he said, abruptly resentful of the way she held him here, captive in this bed without his clothes, the door locked and the key back in her pocket; these games she seemed to delight in playing with him.

'She stared at him, a mixture of surprise and disappointment in her eyes. "Then I am offended," she said. "We talked about how a good hostess should behave towards her guest, but is it not true that a guest too has duties to perform?"

'She had removed her hand from his chest and opened up a space between them, a movement for which Gavin, in his nakedness, felt relieved.

'"It was not my intention to upset you," he said. "But I think you can allow that I also have duties towards—"

'But she did not allow him to identify them. Removing herself from under the bedcovers, she stood beside him, her gown now belted, her hair shining in the candlelight.

'"Or is it that you lack courage?" She stared at him. "If that's the case, your meeting tomorrow morning doesn't look very promising."

'Gavin did not know how to respond, but then her expression softened.

'"Or do I expect too much? Maybe that's the problem."

She looked into his face. "If nothing else, you might have a keepsake you can give me, something of yours I can remember you by when you are gone?" She paused. "A glove, perhaps?"

'He frowned, telling her he had only one pair of gloves and they were essential for riding his motorcycle in the wintry weather. He sat up.

'"I would love to give you something else, my Lady, but I have nothing with me of any value. Nothing personal. I have brought with me only those things necessary for my journey and my appointment tomorrow morning."

'She came back to the bed and took the ring with the red and green stones from her finger. "Then if you have nothing to give, you can at least take this from me."

'Gavin stared at the beautiful ring and shook his head. "I couldn't possibly accept such a gift," he said. "It's far too valuable and your husband would notice its absence."

'"It was not his gift."

'"I'm sorry, I can't accept it. You must see that."

'"All I see is that you appear unwilling to accept anything I offer you. Anything at all."

'He bowed his head, stung by the truth of what she said. His hands lay on the bedcover like migrating birds stranded on an alien shore. She was standing by the bed, looking down at him.

'"There is one thing, though, that even such a cold-hearted man as you might be willing to take. This belt that ties my gown was woven by my mother. Whoever wears it against their skin will not be harmed by man or beast, or any cunning whatsoever."

'Her words sounded as if they were a part of some old charm, as though she were winding up a spell. Gavin felt drained by the effort of will required to resist each advance she made, but the idea of the belt with its green and gold threads appealed to him, and seemed in keeping with the nature of his quest.

'She sensed his hesitation. "What do you say?" She paused. "Or is the real problem that you dare not be indebted to me, or perhaps to any woman?"

"'I think I could accept such a gift, my Lady."

"'I'm glad of it," she said, "but there are two conditions."

"'Tell me," he said, "though I think I know I am not to tell your husband."

"'Yes," she answered. "That is the first requirement. The second is that you must allow me to tie the belt myself."

"'Then you must give me a moment to put something on."

"'No," she said. "If the belt is to retain its power, you will have to step onto this floor, naked as you are, and let me place it around your waist and tie it tight."

'Gavin sighed inwardly, sensing his powerlessness. "If that is the only way, then so be it," he said.

He pushed away the covers and stood before her.

"'Well," she said, glancing down at him, "I do think you place too much worth on your modesty. In the all-girls school I went to, we learned that in ancient Greece men used to exercise and play sport naked."

"'I learned that too," Gavin answered, "but I also learned in my all-boys school that there were no women present to observe them."

'She took a step towards him and undid her belt so her

gown fell open. She freed it from its loops and put it around Gavin's waist, drawing them together as she pulled it tight and tied the knot. For a moment he recalled his dream in the vixen's cave, when he was a fish with an iron hook in its mouth, being hauled out of the water by a fisher whose face was hidden by a scarf. He could feel the Lady's body against his and stared over her shoulder towards the window, the flickering candles, and the sky that was no longer dark, knowing that her eyes would be searching his for any sign of weakness, knowing that if he allowed her lips to touch his, he would be gone, for her mouth would open and she would swallow him whole.

'She released him and stepped back. "Well, that wasn't so terrible, was it?" She smiled. "And now you have my gift tied around your waist." She paused. "If you show courage tomorrow morning, the power in the belt will keep you from harm."

'She stepped towards him and kissed him lightly on the mouth. "You'll be relieved to know, I'll leave you alone now to get dressed."

'She took the candelabra and crossed the room to the door, but as she reached it, she turned back and looked at him. Gavin had not moved.

'"As my husband insists on teasing you about your uneventful, lazy days in the house, while he is out risking life and limb on the hunt, perhaps we could do something more active on your final morning here?"

'A sense of regret, a feeling of having left something uncompleted, gripped him at the reminder that this would be her last visit to his room. "What do you have in mind, my Lady?"

'"Well, you seem to like challenges."

'Gavin nodded.

'"Can you fire an arrow from a bow and hit the target? A wooden one, of course, stuffed with straw. Nothing that lives and breathes."

'"I can, my Lady. Perhaps we can have a wager for some small token?"

'"You have hit my thought exactly."

'She looked at him, as if about to say something more, but instead she let go of her gown she was holding together with her free hand and reached upwards, as though to brush a strand of hair from her face, or, as she stretched higher, to pluck an apple from an invisible bough. The beltless gown fell open and Gavin saw the whiteness of her breast, he caught a glimpse of russet fur before she drew it together again. She smiled at his confusion.

'"Well, Sir Knight," she said. "Now you have seen everything there is to see. But perhaps you can show me your skill as an archer after breakfast."

'She turned, and taking the key from the pocket of her gown, she slipped it into the lock and opened the door. A moment later she was gone.'

Henley relit his cigar and took a drink. And then we were away again, almost as if he knew as well as I how little time remained to him.

'After he had breakfasted, Gavin sat in the kitchen, expecting the Lady to come and find him, but she did not appear. Wondering if there had been a misunderstanding, he put on his jacket and followed the passage from the kitchen to the side entrance he had entered by on the first morning.

But before he had opened the door, he could tell where she was and what she was doing by the thud of her arrows as they struck the two targets on the lawn in front of the house. He crossed the gravel until he was close enough to watch. She appeared unaware of his presence and continued to shoot at the target, which was bristling with the arrows she had already fired.

'He had not taken much notice when he had seen her the first afternoon, but he saw now the easy motion of her arm as she reached into the quiver slung over her shoulder and lined the arrow up against the wooden bow. He watched her draw back the string and sensed the strength in her arm as she pulled it taut, before releasing her grip and letting the arrow fly towards the target's circular heart. Unnerved by her seeming mastery of the world around her, and realising that once again he might not be a match for her, Gavin stepped forward.

'Hearing his approach, she turned and greeted him, as though they had not lain in the same bed together within the last two hours with only a scrap of silk between them. Her hair was tied in a red scarf and she was wearing boots, jeans and a tight-fitting leather jacket. On the grass beside her he saw another bow and a full quiver.

'"You seem to have me at a disadvantage."

'"Why's that?"

'"Because you've been here practising, while I was having breakfast. It's also been a while since I've done any archery."

'"It sounds like you're getting your excuses in early," she said. "You don't need to worry. I'm not that good, and you can have some practice while I go back to the house to find a prize for this wager of ours."

'She went to collect her arrows and Gavin picked up the bow he was to use. It was the same as hers, a traditional English longbow without any modern fittings. He tested the tension in the string and wondered if he could possibly beat her when he had not used one for years. She came back from the target and handed him her arrows.

'"Use your time well." She smiled, and walked off towards the house.

'By the time she returned, his arm was aching from the unaccustomed strain on his muscles. However, he felt more confident as he pulled his last arrows from the target and made his way towards her. She held out her hand, in which a gold coin rested. Its edges were worn from long use.

'"This is the prize," she said. "A family heirloom, and worth something, I suspect. But as you will presumably give it to my husband this evening if you win, there's no risk of it passing into a stranger's possession."

'Happy she did not object to him having nothing to wager in return, Gavin nodded in agreement and bent to examine what she held, but her fingers closed around it.

'"Oh no, you can only look if you win."

'"I wondered whose head was on it, and if there was a date. It interests me to know how old it is."

'"Oh, it's old," she said. "Older than this house, older than the foundations, and they're medieval."

'She put the coin in her pocket and looked at him. "Let's begin. Three arrows or six?"

'"Six. It hardly seems worth it otherwise."

'"Fine. But as my guest, you shoot first." And as Gavin

opened his mouth to protest, she shook her head. "No discussion," she said. "That's the way it is. You must know there are rules to every sport, and these ones are mine."

'Gavin put five arrows in his quiver and then lined up the sixth. He sensed the chill of the morning, which a watery sun was unable to disperse. Behind the two targets with their concentric rings of white, black, blue and red, and the circle of gold at the heart, were the wooded hills where the Green Chapel lay waiting. As he drew back the string for his first shot, he sensed her step closer and felt her breath on his cheek.

'"Have you placed the cock where it should be, Sir Knight?"

'He relaxed his grip and turned to look at her. Her face was close to his and her eyes were full of secret laughter.

'"The cock feathers?"

'"What else?"

'"I've forgotten how one's supposed to do it."

'"They should be at right angles to the notch – I mean, the nock." She kept her eyes on his, holding his gaze. "Though, I'm told that some archers like to shoot with the cock up."

'Gavin closed his eyes and turned away from her. He tried to push her whispering out of his mind and focus on what he was aiming at. "The target on the left?"

'"Yes."

'He let go of the arrow and watched it fly.

'And so they shot their arrows, and no matter which ring Gavin's struck, the Lady matched him, ring for ring, colour for colour. With only one shot left, they went to inspect the target to check that what they saw from a distance was indeed the case. It was: they each had one black, three blue and one red.

'"This time, to win the gold, we must hit the gold," she said.

'"But what if it's still a tie? I'm sure you wouldn't want to divide the prize in two?"

'She shook her head. "We would have to keep shooting one arrow at a time until someone won. Sudden death. But I don't want us to stay out here all morning. Your time is short, and I've asked Lukas to bring us coffee in the library as usual. I feel sure that with the final arrow one of us will break the deadlock."

'Gavin nodded and took aim once more. He stared down the line of the shaft at the target's golden heart. His arm was tired, and it was difficult to hold the bow steady. He released the bowstring and watched the arrow bury its head in the red ring. Disappointed, he stepped back to give the Lady room and watched as she lined up the target. He saw the outline of her breast as she drew back her arm, the way her body tensed like a young deer about to jump a stream as she took aim, and how at the last moment her bow appeared to swing to the right and the arrow sped towards a different destination.

'"Well," she said. "You can see I've hit the gold – only in the wrong target. How foolish of me. That means you've beaten me, Sir Knight. I offer you my congratulations."

'She leaned forward to kiss him, slipping the gold coin, his winnings, into his palm at the same time. And there was nothing he could say.'

Henley paused to take another drink, but the interruption was momentary. I marvelled at the way he was able to keep the story unwinding before us. A story whose ending I was beginning to doubt he would ever have time to reach.

'They were sitting in the chairs that had grown familiar in the quiet of the library,' Henley went on. 'Their coffee cups were empty, and the book lay open before them. Gavin was gazing at a watercolour of a fox standing at the edge of a wintry forest, one paw raised to continue its journey. But it had caught the scent of something, and was poised now between one moment and the next. He saw its thick winter coat and creamy breast, the red brush that trailed in the snow. Bright eyes stared out at him, watching and waiting.

'"Sly old Reynard," he heard her whisper beside him. "You can almost see the thoughts flicker behind his eyes." She paused. "Except that perhaps this one is not the dog fox at all, but his mate, the vixen. And she's more cunning still."

'Gavin watched her hand cover his beside the open page. He saw the gold ring with its red and green stones, which he had refused; he saw the bracelet with its charm. Her leg pressed against his beneath the table. She was very close to him and he feared if he turned his head, her lips would open and he would be in danger once more.

'"I must be stupid," he said, his eyes looking into the vixen's. "I've just realised we've been following the three hunts ourselves from the quiet of this room – deer, boar, fox."

'"Of course," she answered softly. "I'm surprised it's taken you so long to notice."

'Puzzled, he turned towards her. Her eyes were smiling and her lips invited him.

'Behind them the door opened with a bang and Bertilak's voice filled the library.

'"Sorry to interrupt things, but it's been a damn frustrating morning!"

'They looked at him, his hunting clothes stained and muddy, his face ruddy from the chase. Gavin had been so preoccupied, he had not heard the hunters' return. Neither of them moved.

'"Empty-handed, young fellow! Quite empty-handed! Not like yesterday or the day before. Never known anything like it." He held his arms out. "We chased a fox all morning, hounds panting and slobbering and howling. Sometimes he was ahead of us, sometimes behind us, but whenever we caught sight of him, he didn't seem out of breath at all, as if he had all the time in the world, as though our attempts to catch him were part of a game he was playing."

'"Or possibly, *she* was playing," the Lady added.

'Bertilak's glance seemed to fall upon them directly for the first time and Gavin suffered the embarrassment of knowing his wife had not removed her hand from his.

'Bertilak shrugged. "Perhaps, but whatever sex the creature had, the cunning brute outfoxed us all. He, or she, is probably sitting under a tree somewhere at this moment, with a grin as wide as the ocean on their wretched face."

'He looked at them and seemed to cheer up. "But perhaps you've already been more successful, my young friend. We'll see each other at dinner."

'And with a wave, he turned and left them.'

As Henley reached for his glass, I heard footsteps coming down the stairs and looked to see that Phelbas had finally grown tired of waiting and was standing by the door, his impatience visible. I glanced back at Henley and then held up five fingers to Phelbas. In five minutes we would move upstairs and see if the story could be completed there. Phelbas nodded, but did not move, as though he no longer trusted my ability to keep my word. And as I looked at him, standing at the back of the saloon, I wondered what he thought of our storytelling, our bundles of words that for most of us took the place of the kind of life he had been leading, in places remote and strange, for years past counting.

'Dinner was finished – another serving of the wild boar they had eaten the previous evening. It was New Year's Eve, you must remember,' Henley continued, 'just like tonight.'

He gave the saloon one of his sweeping glances, like a lighthouse beam falling on every face, to see if we were alert and listening.

'This is a story for New Year, after all.'

Which I had managed to forget. Perhaps, despite the tale's extraordinary length, that was all the reason there was for him telling it tonight, and my feeling that there must be some deeper cause, that this was the story he had always wanted to tell, was unwarranted.

'Gavin sat waiting for Bertilak's description of the day's hunt and the ritual exchange of winnings. He wondered how his host would present the morning's failure. At least he would have more than kisses to offer on this last occasion. He took out the gold coin and tried to decipher the inscriptions. He didn't know anything about old coins, but it looked well cared for and he supposed it might be on display in some part of the house he had not been shown.

'"That looks a beauty. Would you let me see it?"

'Gavin passed it to his neighbour, a middle-aged man wearing a red bow tie. The dress of his much younger blonde companion was of a similar colour.

'"Is it yours?"

'"Only for a few hours. I'm returning it to Lord Bertilak, Bertie, in a moment – it's a long story."

'His neighbour smiled. "Most good ones usually are."

'The man held it up to the light and rolled it in his hand, and Gavin had a momentary fear he was in the company of a magician who would cause the coin to disappear between his fingers, even while he stared at it. But the man placed it on the bare oak of the table and took a small magnifying glass from his pocket.

'"I'm a collector. I can tell you about it, if you like."

'"I'd be most interested."

'"It's a gold noble, a fine example. Over six hundred years old. Very rare and worth a lot of money."

'"Can you tell when it was minted?"

'"Well, that looks like Richard II on the obverse – the inscription round the edge identifies him as Richard – and the girlish face certainly doesn't belong to Richard the Lionheart or Richard III. That would make it the second half of the fourteenth century. The reverse is curious, and shows an armed and helmeted knight holding a tree in his gloved hand. No words to explain anything." He put his magnifying glass away and looked at Gavin. "Are you sure you have to return it to Bertie? I'd give you a good price."

'Gavin shook his head. "Quite sure, I'm afraid."

'A glass was being banged on the table and Gavin turned to find his host was on his feet, ready to describe the pursuit of the fox that had outwitted them all, hounds included, that morning. Gavin watched the Lady, who sat tonight at her husband's side. She was wearing a cream-coloured dress that hung from her bare shoulders, and each piece of jewellery he had grown familiar with was plain to see. And though his coming ordeal droned in the background, his thoughts revolved around her and the way she had beguiled him when her husband was out hunting.

'To a more subdued round of applause than usual, his host completed the account of the unsuccessful hunt and, in the same instant, his wife stood up and left the table. Gavin realised she had not been present once at the exchange of winnings.

'Bertilak was looking in his direction, and he got to his feet and crossed the hall. He was greeted with a hug.

'"As you know, I have nothing to show for all my efforts today."

'"You told me at the start that our little agreement is not a competition," Gavin said. "You know it doesn't matter. Especially when my winnings have always been so poor in contrast to yours."

'He paused, enjoying this small sense of triumph, before stepping forward and kissing Bertilak three times, lightly, on the lips. The Lady's kisses had certainly lingered longer and he wondered if there had been more than three, but he felt sure their symbolic significance was enough. As on the previous evening, a hush settled over the dining hall as the guests watched.

'"Is that all?" Bertilak asked.

'Gavin shook his head. "Not today," he said, and taking the coin from his pocket, he placed it in his host's hand. Bertilak seemed surprised as he examined it.

'"It looks familiar," he said.

'"That's not for me to say. You know our rules: there is no obligation to explain how the winnings were gained."

'Bertilak nodded and the two men stood studying each other, as though each had something else he might have said. The hall was quiet and filled with an air of anticipation. Abruptly, Bertilak held out his hand.

'"I wish you all the best for the morning," he said. "I'm sure you'll be able to fulfil whatever task awaits you as steadfastly and honestly as you have kept to the terms of our agreement here." He lowered his voice. "Someone will be waiting in the morning to guide you, as I promised." He gripped Gavin's hand tighter. "Come back for breakfast when you're finished. We can say goodbye to each other properly then – or, who knows, you might even decide to stay on a while longer. You'd be more than welcome."

'He released Gavin with a smile and the latter returned to his seat, the soft touch of the Lady's belt against his skin reminding him of the promise to his host that he had failed to keep, the agreement he had broken.'

Henley paused for a drink and I kept my gaze away from Phelbas standing in the doorway. I hoped the five minutes had not yet passed.

'Midnight came, the Lady returned, and they all linked

arms and sang *Auld Lang Syne* and toasted the New Year, though Gavin found it hard to simulate the merriment of the other guests. Not long afterwards, he made his excuses and followed the long passageway that led to his chamber in the tower. At the foot of the staircase, he saw the glow from her candle and felt his heart quicken, though he did not understand how she could have got there before him.

"'I thought you might need something to light your way to bed,' she said, as she repeated the formula and led him up the stairs. As on the previous nights, she opened the chamber door for him and stood back to let him enter.

"'I didn't see you leave the hall after the singing,' Gavin said, worried his voice would betray the emotions that threatened to get the better of him.

"'I'm the lady of the house,' she answered. "I come and go as I please. But I am glad we have the chance to say our farewells now."

'The candlelight fell upon her face and hair, the pearl that rested in the hollow of her throat. He felt his body stiffen as they stood so close together and he moved his left hand towards the fingers of her free hand. But before he could touch her, she kissed her fingertips and brushed his lips with them. She looked straight into his eyes.

"'You are outside the rules of your wager now, Sir Knight,' she said. "In one respect that might lead you to think you can earn another kiss from me, perhaps even more, and let it remain a secret between us. But you have already hidden something of your winnings from my husband. It might not be advisable to risk another transgression, not when you face such a stern test in the morning."

'Gavin felt his cheeks burn at her words. Her gold wedding ring was visible where her hand gripped the candlestick, and he wondered if she took pleasure in leading him on like this, if that was what she was doing.

'"You're right," he said. "I apologise."

'She gave a smile and her eyes shone. "Oh, Sir Knight, you have no need to apologise. If ever anyone behaved like a gentleman, it has been you." She took his hand in hers. "But it's time to say goodbye, at least until tomorrow when your ordeal will be over."

'For an instant she tightened her fingers, but before he had a chance to say anything further, she turned and started to descend the spiral stairs. The candlelight diminished and vanished, and with a heavy heart he entered his room.

'He undressed, trying to keep thoughts of the morning at bay. Turning back the sheets he found his pyjamas were still missing, but it no longer mattered. The Lady would not visit him in the morning, so he could sleep naked without fear of embarrassment; he would leave the belt around his waist as she had instructed and perhaps, though he did not really believe it, there would be time for it to fill him with some of its supposed powers.

'She was in his head now, and he realised with a shock that since his arrival, he had spent more time thinking about her than the quest, which was his reason for being here. She was a married woman, at least ten years older than him, and he was a guest whom her husband had befriended. But he found to his dismay that none of these things seemed to matter. He ached for her, and he didn't know if this was love or something less worthy, or the consequences of some spell she had woven. And what did she think of him? She had squeezed his fingers as though he meant something to her, but she had also teased and flirted with him mercilessly.

'Gavin turned out the light and listened to the world outside his head. Beyond the stone walls of his castle tower, an owl was hunting its prey through the chill night air; he heard it call, he imagined the silent swoop of its wings as, talons outstretched, it snatched some creature from the earth's uplifted face.'

The Green Chapel

Henley's voice faltered and he stopped, and for the first time I thought he looked drained by all this storytelling. As on that earlier occasion when his voice had wavered, he rested a hand on the back of a chair to steady himself and I saw him looking at Lovell's cousin. Her face was full of concern, but she wasn't the only one. I heard voices whispering to him, asking if he was all right. He took a deep breath and nodded. He was still for long seconds, as though drawing on some inner source of strength. But as he straightened up again, I got to my feet, needing no further gesture of impatience from Phelbas standing in the doorway to tell me what I needed to do. After apologising to Henley for the interruption, I explained the situation and reminded them all of the traditional course of the evening, which involved toasting the Barrier as we steamed through it. I made clear it would be possible to hear the completion of Henley's tale, however, as there was seating in the covered part of the stern.

'But it'll be cold up there,' someone grumbled.

'We've all seen the bloody Barrier, anyway,' the Interrupter added.

But I was prepared for the complaints, and there were also voices of support. It was Henley himself who decided the matter.

'I'm also a believer in keeping traditions alive,' he said, 'and I'm in need of some fresh air, so I'm perfectly willing to complete my little tale—'

'Little?!' Beddoes spluttered over the glass of wine he was drinking.

'…on deck.' Henley stood there surveying us, as he had done throughout the evening. 'Always assuming that the company has not grown tired of hearing my old voice droning on.'

The remark was unnecessary, but before anyone could offer the encouragement Henley appeared to need, I saw Lovell's cousin get to her feet.

'I think there's no one present who doesn't wish to hear the end of your story,' she said, her eyes resting on his. 'But a short break does seem like a good idea. You must be exhausted having to remember so many details. What Gavin and the Lady were wearing, or not wearing, for instance.' She smiled. 'I've never had such a tale told to me in my life before.'

He seemed taken aback by her words, but he gave her a little bow and then, to a gentle round of applause which might partly have been for her, we began to make our way upstairs.

The relocation went more smoothly than I had anticipated. As we cast off from our moorings in Greenwich and Phelbas steered the *Astarte* back out into the river, the company reassembled on what would have been the sun deck in the summer months. Rows of wooden seats faced the stern, where there was room for everyone, and though a glass roof provided some protection from the wind, most had fetched their coats. Not Henley, however, who placed a chair for himself out in the open against the taffrail, where it was sure to be windy. He had fastened his jacket and found a woollen scarf to tie around his neck. And that was all. I watched him as he stood leaning over the rail, puffing on a cigar and looking back towards the City beyond the bend in the river.

Phelbas told me that after passing through the Barrier, which we would reach soon, he would keep to our traditional routine, despite it being later than usual, and steam downriver for a couple of miles before turning round. He hoped this would give Henley enough time to finish. I nodded in agreement. It would be well after midnight before we got back, but a few fireworks missed was preferable to arriving at Swan Lane Steps with the ending of the story unheard. That seemed unlikely, however. From what I could recall of the original poem on which Henley's tale appeared to be based, despite his insistence on his account being true, we had reached the fourth and final *fitt*, which I imagined might be called *The Green Chapel*.

I took the opportunity to ask Phelbas about the weather, but he shrugged, saying that the shipping forecast for the North Sea and the Thames Estuary had mentioned unusual wind patterns, but they were too far away to concern us. We both gazed up at the night sky and I saw nothing alarming there, though the heavy clouds had returned.

'What about your fears of winds from the Russian steppes?'

A faint smile lit his dark features. 'I'm sure they'll arrive – but later than I anticipated.'

And that was how we left it. I trusted his judgement. He was a Phoenician sea captain, after all.

I sensed a growing hush at my back and saw that Henley was looking at me. I turned my head and found the company was waiting. Fresh air had been breathed, new bottles opened, and I noticed that the two women were now sitting near the front. For a moment I thought Henley was about to speak to them, but they were deep in conversation and he must have changed his mind. I had stationed myself in an end seat, where Phelbas could speak to me easily if it were necessary. I wondered if Henley would need a moment to regain his footing, but I needn't have worried. As the Isle of Dogs slid into our wake, he returned us in confident tones to that chamber in the tower where Gavin slept. Except, we learned, he hadn't.

'Gavin did not sleep,' Henley said. Though he had a chair beside him, he was still standing, his face lit by the glow of the *Astarte*'s lamps, while behind him, in the darkness, the river unwound. 'The alarm he had set was not necessary, and when his clock told him it was time, he lit some candles he had found in a drawer to remind him of the Lady's three early-morning visits. Placing them on the window ledge, he watched their flames bending as the wind gusted outside, where it would be cold, where the sun had not yet risen, and it was midwinter.

'When he was dressed, he sat on the bed, his gauntlets, helmet, and the gold bar in its cloth of velvet beside him, and stared at the reflections of the flames in the glass. He was waiting for it to be light enough to go downstairs and take his Triumph from the stable, and he wondered who Lord Bertilak had told to show him the way to the Green Chapel. Lukas, perhaps? Or, the stray thought entered his head, might the guide even be Bertilak himself?

'The castle, as he now imagined it, was quiet. The last Old Year hunt was over, and everyone would be sleeping. Gavin wondered if his body had absorbed any of the life-preserving powers of the belt the Lady had given him, and he imagined her now, her long, chestnut hair spread dreamlike over the pillow, Lord Bertilak breathing deeply beside her. The picture shocked him – where else would she sleep but at her husband's side?

'He heard a door bang downstairs and footsteps crossing the gravel. It must be time for him to leave. He did not want to keep his guide waiting outside in the cold, but now that the moment had arrived, he wondered if he had the courage to submit to the terms of the challenge and keep his side of the agreement. Who would fault him if he crept out of the house, started the Triumph, and headed back to London and the everyday world? No one would know. Except himself. He, Gavin, would know. Always.

'He blew out the candles and opened the window. The sky behind the mountain was a pearly grey and the stars had gone. The frozen water encircling the house glittered like the Lady's silver necklace, and the moon hung low over the bony mountainside towards which he would be riding. He would go and get the motorcycle ready. He could not turn back.

'The stone stairs echoed as he descended; the walls of the passage to the hall, where they had all said goodbye the previous night and wished him good health for the New Year, gave back the sounds of his footsteps. The lamps gleamed, electric current flowed as usual through the veins of the building, but he was the only one moving through the cold and silent rooms and he could not prevent the melancholy notion that they had already forgotten him. She too, despite the fact that he wore her belt against his skin. No one had taken the trouble to forsake the warmth of their bed to give him a last wave of the hand.

'He left the house by the side door and walked round to the stables. The day that was not yet day was raw and the wind stung his eyes as it scoured the outbuildings. He repacked the gold bar in a saddlebag and would have liked to start the engine, as hearing the steady beat it had rediscovered since he had cleaned the carburettors would have been reassuring, but he did not wish to draw attention to his departure before it was necessary. He could feel the sun climbing unseen behind the mountain as the moon sank, and he wondered where his guide was. He wanted to be at the chapel by sunrise and could not delay leaving much longer. Realising he was shivering, and not certain if it was from the cold alone, he wheeled the motorcycle out of the stable and mounted it. He looked around, but could see no one. The windows of the house were dark. He put on his helmet and gloves and, raising himself high in the saddle, he kicked down with his right leg. He did it a second time, and then at the third attempt the engine came to life. He sat in the saddle, coaxing the machine with the throttle, feeling its regular throb. Then he engaged the clutch and rolled forward.

'"Hello!"

'He stopped and turned to find a boy in an old pullover that was several sizes too large for him, standing there.

'"Father told me you needed someone to show you the way. To the chapel."

'Gavin nodded, surprised to discover that Lord Bertilak had a son. "And is that someone you?"

"'Yes."

'Gavin stared at him sceptically. The boy didn't fit his picture of how a lord's son should look. "Haven't you got a helmet?"

"'I won't need one. Besides, I fall lightly."

"'I hope that won't be necessary. Get up behind me, then."

'He felt the boy's arms round his waist.

"'You're quite sure you know where to go?"

"'Of course. Cross the bridge and then turn right along the track through the fields. Keep going until you reach the stream that comes off the mountain. I'll tell you when we get there."

'Gavin nodded and pulled down his visor. He had not seen the boy before and wondered why his existence had never been mentioned. They rode across the gravel and over the stream that encircled the house. As Gavin looked down, he saw the water was still frozen, but now he had the impression that he could see pale faces, their features pinched with the cold, staring up at him, while hands, bony and white, pressed against the ice in their efforts to free themselves. He shivered at the tricks imagination could play, and turned in the direction the boy had indicated.

'He drove slowly over the rough track, the headlamp's beam still necessary in the pale light. Above the noise of the engine, he heard an owl hoot and saw it glide across the frozen fields where no animals grazed, to land at the top of an isolated oak tree. Three crows rose from the bare branches, cawing and complaining, their hoarse cries filling the air.

'The boy's grip tightened. "Stop here."

'Gavin braked and waited. To their left a stream, that seemed strangely silent, glinted as it tumbled over the rocks. The boy dismounted and pointed to a path that led upwards, before losing itself among grey boulders.

'"The place you're looking for is on the other side of the mountain. It's not far and this path will take you straight there. You won't miss it." His eyes strayed over the Triumph. "You'll have to leave the motorbike here, though. It'll be waiting when you get back." He looked at Gavin. "But maybe you won't come back."

'"What do you mean?"

'"Some people say there's a devil or a monster that lives in the rocks up by the chapel. I don't believe it, but I wouldn't go up there on my own, especially not on certain days of the year like today. Father says you must be a bit crazy to want to meet someone there." He paused. "Why don't you forget about it and come home and have breakfast? We could ride further down the track to the lake so it'll look like you've tried to find this person, and then, when we get home, you can say there was no one there. I won't say anything, so no one will ever know."

'Gavin shook his head. "Thanks for your concern," he said, "but I've come too far to back out now. Besides, it's a commitment I've made. I think one should stick to those, don't you?"

'He looked at the boy, dressed in the shapeless woollen pullover that might have belonged to his father; it hung on the slender frame he had inherited from his mother like a blanket on a clothes hanger. His presence, this reminder of his parents' union, unsettled Gavin and he found it difficult to decide how old the boy was.

'"I suppose so," the boy said. "It's the kind of thing we get told at school."

'"Well, thanks for bringing me here."

'Gavin held out his hand. The boy shook it and cast another look at the motorcycle.

'"Do you think I could have the Triumph if you don't come back?"

'Gavin stared at him. "Don't worry, I'm quite certain I'll be coming back."

'"But if you don't?" the boy persisted.

'"If I don't come back," Gavin said, after a pause, "it's yours, though I think you're too young to ride it."

'The boy grinned. "Thank you. I can get to know how everything works until I'm old enough to ride it, though as this is private land, the law doesn't apply here."

'They said goodbye. Gavin turned to watch him as he started his walk back down the track towards the house, and wondered uneasily which law in particular didn't apply on Lord Bertilak's land. He got off the motorcycle and wheeled it onto the grass. Removing the gold bar in its wrapper from the saddlebag, he surveyed the Triumph as if this might indeed be the last time he saw it. He took his glove off and rubbed his hand over the fuel tank with the silver pentangle he had drawn, so long ago it now seemed. He closed his eyes and felt the raised threads of the silver paint, as though he were reading something inscribed in

Braille, as though it were a mnemonic he needed to help him focus on the task ahead. A, G, C, M and C: the Axe he had encountered once; the Gold he held in his hand; he was still Chaste, having resisted with growing reluctance the Lady's temptations; the Motorcycle stood before him; and only the Chapel and the second encounter with the Axe were still to be faced. All that remained was to follow the path the boy had indicated over the shoulder of the mountain, between the grey rocks to where the Green Chapel and its guardian must be waiting.

'He hesitated. It was too absurd. The year was 1963. This wasn't the Middle Ages, yet here he was trembling in fear of a green man who had threatened to behead him if he failed to meet the terms of a bargain they had made in the city of London a year before. The boy had spoken of a devil, a monster who lived by the Chapel. Did either of them really believe this?'

'My thoughts exactly,' I heard the Interrupter break in. 'Do any of us really believe this story that Henley claims to be true? It's what I've said before.'

'And what the rest of us have said to you before,' the Bulldog growled, 'is to let the story be told. You can argue about its truth or untruth afterwards, if you still want to. It's not important now.'

I feared Henley might be drawn into the argument, as he had insisted that his tale was a true one, but he chose to ignore the interruption, his eyes remaining fixed on some invisible point above our heads that he had been addressing for most of the evening. I had the feeling his only desire now was to reach the end of the narrative and sit down. A chorus of voices called for quiet and Henley returned us to Gavin's moment of doubt.

'It seemed he had become a protagonist in an old story. He took a deep breath and zipped his jacket up tighter against the cold. The sooner he got this thing over, the better. He removed his silver helmet and hung it over the handlebars; he took out the key that would lock the front wheel and the uncertainty returned. It would not be so simple for the boy to retrieve the Triumph if he secured it, but to leave it unlocked, or with the key in the lock, even, would imply he had no faith in the outcome of his meeting. And he did believe he would be riding the motorcycle again before the morning was over. With a decisive movement he turned the key and put it in his pocket. Then he started up the path beside the stream.'

The *Astarte* had been losing speed and I heard the sound of the steamer's engines change as we began to pass through the Barrier and the noise bounced back from the concrete piers. Up behind us in the wheelhouse, the ship's radio crackled. I watched the steel domes housing the hydraulic cylinders, which rotated the gates into position when the Barrier closed, slide past. Amber warning lights were blinking, and I had the feeling we were abandoning a place of safety as we left the City's limits behind us; as though we were crossing a drawbridge that would be raised as soon as we had passed over. But perhaps the details of Henley's story were playing tricks on me.

Henley had paused and decided to sit down, as we gazed at the Barrier and the row of lights that flickered across the width of the river like orange flame. I turned to see if

Phelbas would appear to offer an explanation, and saw him coming towards me. He beckoned and, while heads turned to watch our progress and some of the company followed the tradition and raised their glasses, I followed him back down the deck.

'No need for alarm,' he said. 'The Barrier will be closed at low tide in two to three hours, because of a possible storm surge. By then, we'll be safely back home.'

'Isn't there any danger at all?'

He shook his head. 'You know I wouldn't risk the lives of passengers, or the *Astarte*. All will be well. But I'll only take us as far as Woolwich Reach and then turn round.'

Trusting his judgement, I nodded.

'This way, everyone can enjoy going through the Barrier, and I can taste some real sea salt on my lips that you only get once you leave the Barrier behind. You know, I don't get many chances these days.'

So that was the reason for not turning back early, I thought, as I returned to my seat. Phelbas' weakness for the taste of sea salt on his lips was not on the standard list of vices, but it was an interesting confession.

'As he followed the stream higher, Gavin began to understand its silence,' Henley resumed, once I had passed on the news to the company and allayed some concerns about our safety. 'Shards of ice hung from the rocks, and though it appeared that water still trickled downwards beneath a frozen canopy, its sound was sealed away. But this evidence of a cold early morning in January barely penetrated his thoughts, which were preoccupied with the memory of a severed head that bounced and rolled among the chairs and tables of a New Year's Eve celebration dinner; a head that was then grasped by its owner, a hugely unlikely green stranger, so it could remind Gavin not to forget his appointment on this very day, at this very hour.

'The path turned away from the stream and, as it crossed the mountain's shoulder, the ground vanished. Startled by the transformation of the landscape, Gavin halted and gazed down at the dark shadows of a gorge into which the track would lead him. Above his head, the sky was lightening. The frayed edges of the scattered clouds were beginning to catch fire and, as he turned to the east, the first rays of the sun struck him in the face. The light, the faint warmth from a source so distant, gave him heart, but in the same moment a sound from the gorge below caused him to recoil in shock.

'*Thwaaack!*

'Gavin stared into the gloomy depths where the sun's light would not shine for a while yet, but could see nothing.

'*Thwaaack!*

'The grating, grinding sound scraped the air even louder than before. It raised the hairs on his scalp and made him grit his teeth. He knew it was the noise of iron being dragged across stone; the sound an axe blade would make when it was sharpened on a lathe.

'*Thwaaack!*

'Gavin gazed, wide-eyed, into the gorge, but saw only rocks, some twisted trees and a grassy mound at the far end. It was the most unwelcome noise he had ever heard, but it was also the reason he had come to this desolate place. Clutching the gold bar to his chest, he began to descend the path.

'By the time he reached level ground, the noise had ceased. No birds sang, no small creature scuttled in the bracken. The only sound to be heard came from water tumbling down the side of the cliffs that rose on either side of the strange mound. He looked around him and saw how the gorge was wider than he had imagined, the sides edged with jagged rocks that, like sharp, uneven teeth, lined the jaws of the sprung trap he had entered. He felt this was the place he had been expected to find, but where was the Green Chapel? Where was Greneknighte, whom he had come so far to meet?

'He began to walk towards the mound. The sky above his head might soon be blue, but he followed the overgrown track among shadows. The grass underfoot was rimed with frost and his breath hung about his head like a shroud. He walked steadily, his heart thudding in his chest, the gold heavy in his hand. As he approached the tumulus, he saw there was an opening to which the path led. It seemed to be an entrance, though long tendrils of ivy partly obscured it. Moss and grass covered the rocks; a holly bush, thick with blood-red berries, stood upon the summit. And the water fell unceasingly down the face of the cliff, splashing into a pool he could not see.

'Gavin stood outside the gap in the rocks that opened into the dark. He was sure this was the place and it was 'green' only in the sense that it was natural. He wondered if he was expected to go inside; if that was where Greneknighte would be waiting for him. His body shaking, he stepped towards the entrance and squeezed between the rocks that were worn smooth, as though by the passage of many bodies.

He was anticipating darkness, but discovered instead a kind of cave, something that might once have been a hermit's cell, filled with a grey light that entered down a rock chimney. Water dripped, and the space was full of the smell of damp leaves and colourless shoots, of things growing upwards towards the sun. He looked round him, half expecting to find evidence of human occupation – signs on the walls, carvings, a primitive altar – but there was nothing. He stood in the pool of light, listening to the soft plash of water, the whisperings of plants, dreading any moment to have his shoulder grasped by a gloved hand, to hear his name being called.

'*Thwaaack!*

'A pause.

'*Thwaaack!*

'Another pause.

'*Thwaaack!*

'A silence in which the air rang with the sound of iron grinding against stone, filling the hollow under the earth where Gavin stood trembling, penetrating each soft recess of his being.

'The echoes faded, and Gavin imagined his antagonist running a thumb along the edge of his axe to see if it might be sharp enough to shave with. He heard footsteps, and then the voice.

'"You can't skulk in there, you know! A sharpened blade will grow blunt with waiting. Come out so we can complete the terms of our contract."'

Henley surveyed his audience once more, as he had done all evening. Everyone was still on board, so to speak, and though Phelbas had wanted us up on deck so we might see the Barrier from close quarters, all anyone seemed to want to do was sit on the hard benches in this covered part of the deck and listen as the story drew to its conclusion. And Henley sat perched in the stern, a beer glass on a table he had procured from somewhere, like a prophet from the past, an old philosopher who has foresuffered all, dressed in a black suit with a woollen scarf wrapped around his neck.

I saw Lovell raise his hand as if he were in a classroom. Separated from his cousin for the evening, he did not appear to have found any drinking companions to take her place and had looked ill at ease whenever my eyes chanced to fall on him.

'Great story, Mr Henley. First-class entertainment. I don't recall hearing a better.'

I liked his enthusiasm, and I suppose, as a librarian, the nature of the story was bound to appeal to him, but this wasn't the time to be paying compliments. That could all be done when we got back

'Much obliged to you, I'm sure,' Henley responded. 'To be perfectly honest, I'm rather embarrassed by how long the thing is taking to tell. It doesn't seem to want to come to an end.'

Lovell nodded. 'Let's hope you manage it before next year's outing, though.'

They laughed at this, though I didn't find it so amusing. 'If you don't mind, I've got a quick question.'

Henley seemed surprised by the interruption, when time was running out on us, and I glared at Lovell, furious that he had decided to ask something when we were almost home and dry. But Henley was as polite as ever.

'Ask away.'

'The sound of the axe blade being sharpened. This "*Thwaaack*" that you pronounce so effectively. I mean, how does one write that on the page?'

Henley looked at him a moment. 'It's not on a page,' he said. 'It's not written down anywhere.'

Lovell looked puzzled, but before he could reply, another voice hijacked the discussion.

'So where did you get the story from, Henley?' It was the Interrupter.

There was a long pause, and I could see a universe of textual authenticity issues opening up before us again. But Henley's insistence on the truth of the tale had led to this moment.

'From the great man himself,' he said finally.

'The oral tradition, so to speak,' I interposed, anxious to forestall any discussion on the implications of Henley's answer.

The Interrupter ignored me. 'Which must mean that our gallant hero survived the ordeal he is about to face. So no more suspense, Henley. That certainly is a spoiler. Maybe we don't need to hear any more.'

Henley looked taken aback by the rudeness of the remark. I was about to step in and say something, but the Bulldog was quicker.

'Maybe *you* don't need to hear any more! Why don't you go and sit in the bow and spare us from having to listen to any more of your comments?'

The Interrupter got unsteadily to his feet – he'd clearly had a few glasses of something – and looked for Henley's champion, but he was pulled back down by those sitting closest to him. To my surprise, I even saw a fist raised in his direction.

'Maybe it's only Hollywood and bad fiction that think suspense is the most important element in a plot,' I said, wanting to move things on, at the same time aware that my so-called literary snobbery had pitched me into difficulties in the past.

'The way the story unfolds, the characters, the themes, the situation – all these are just as significant as the denouement.' This came from Lovell, who I suspected was regretting his question. I was grateful for his support.

'And, of course, the manner of the telling,' I added, with a look at Henley, who nodded his thanks and took the opportunity to continue.

'Gavin turned and squeezed back into the outside world. The man, almost exactly as he remembered him, was standing by the entrance holding the axe in one hand and the pair of scales in the other. He was dressed in the same green leather suit; he was gloved, booted and helmeted with the visor hiding the upper part of his face. Only the absence of a green beard spreading over his chest made him look in any way different. Even though Gavin could not see his motorcycle – indeed, had not heard an engine, and there appeared to be no way one could be ridden to this place – it seemed as if that was the way he had arrived here.

'"Welcome to the Green Chapel, Sir Gavin," he said, less aggressively than Gavin remembered, bowing his head slightly.

"You are a man of your word and I applaud you for that. You have kept the appointment to the very hour. Come, let's finish this business and then we can go and find somewhere to have a celebratory drink. After all, it is New Year's Day."

'He took a few paces and set the scales down on the ground. Nearby, a squat grey stone seemed to possess the shape and proportions of a chopping block. But not for firewood. Gavin did not understand how Greneknighte could be so sure they would be able to share a drink, though the thought filled him with hope. Perhaps this was only a test of some kind, and by keeping the appointment, he had avoided the moment he had been dreading for a year.

'Greneknighte was using the end of the axe shaft to clear some stones and earth from the base of the squat stone. In a few moments he had uncovered something wrapped in a pale silk cloth. He stooped to pull it out and removed the covering to show Gavin.

'"My half of the bar," he said. "I couldn't be bothered to invest it. Not really my sort of thing, interest rates, dividends, stocks and shares, and counting houses." He looked at Gavin. "I presume you invested yours wisely, so that now, by the terms of our agreement, my return blow will not be necessary."

'Gavin stared at the untouched gold in disbelief, as Greneknighte rubbed a shine into its dull surface with the cloth. Though he had tried to hide the truth from himself during the journey, hoping that perhaps his antagonist had met with similar misfortune in the markets – after all, it had not been a good year for investors – he never dreamed he would have been better advised to do nothing.

'"Let's weigh my bar," he said, his heart trembling.

'Hearing the uncertainty in Gavin's voice, Greneknighte said nothing, but took the gold bar from him and placed it on the ground. He lay his own ingot on the scales and, producing some weights from a pouch he carried, he waited until the two pans were balanced. He read off the weight and asked Gavin to check the figure. Then he replaced his bar with the other. He seemed to take a long time making adjustments, but eventually he looked up at Gavin.

'"Yours is less than mine," he said. "The difference is not great, half a troy ounce, but it nevertheless weighs less. You do not seem to have used your skills as a banker very wisely."

'Gavin nodded, needing no further confirmation of what he knew to be the truth. He felt the familiar world grow cold and empty around him.'

A kind of existential shiver ran through the ranks of evening-dressed men sat listening, and I knew this was the nightmare they could never escape from – the moment the money they had invested on behalf of their clients vanished from the screens in front of them. As though it had never existed. I had seen them in their offices, staring at the columns of numbers that flickered before their eyes: the prices of oil and butter, timber and tea, the magical ranks of green, blue and red figures; and with a twitch of the wrist they bought or sold. But it was like clutching at the colours of a rainbow – it was never money; they were not dealing with the piles of notes a clerk used to tally in those counting houses Greneknighte so contemptuously referred to. There were no bags of gold any more that Phelbas' ancestors might have crossed the Mediterranean to earn by trading cedar wood; they had long since vanished and in their place was a world whose existence you could not quite guarantee, because it functioned like the electrical impulses inside your own mind and might be terminated by a cable being pulled from the wall in a place you were yet to learn of; and these endless streams of figures that passed before their eyes and occupied their days bore no resemblance whatever to the coin you dropped into a beggar's outstretched hand as you passed him on King William Street on the way home from work.

But though the gold had been replaced by currents of electricity, only another form of currency after all, Gavin and Greneknighte stood before us outside the Green Chapel on a cold New Year's Day, two slightly unequal halves of a real gold bar before them, while we all waited to hear what the consequences of the weighing would be. And someone had given me, your Narrator, the task of relating what I saw and heard, what I was witness to, even though the bankers seated around me, Elyssa and Lovell's cousin, Henley, Phelbas and the *Astarte* itself might be no more real than those arrays of figures flashing on the screens in those darkened rooms.

Henley seemed to savour the unease the story had created, for he sat there listening to the whispering from his seat in the stern, a faint smile playing on his lips. And as the river widened and Phelbas turned the wheel so the *Astarte* could describe an arc that would bring her round and we could start the journey home, I felt the savour of salt on my lips, exactly as the Phoenician had promised; the taste of sea salt but a scent of something else too, some intermingling of earth and water, something primitive that seemed to be rolling through the night towards us. I stared into the darkness of the estuary, but saw nothing strange, and though the wind blew stronger, everyone else was preoccupied with the climax of the story that Henley seemed to have reached. I watched him take a sip of beer before resuming his tale.

'Leaving the two halves of the gold bar on the ground beside the scales, Greneknighte rose to his feet. "It seems we must return to the terms of our agreement," he said, taking hold of the axe from where it had been resting against the stone. "A blow for a blow, if you remember. Both halves of the ingot return to me also."

'"I remember the terms very well," Gavin answered stiffly. It seemed he might have only a few moments of his life before him. He could not believe in his heart that the Lady's belt would save him, and he wondered if he should throw himself upon the green stranger's mercy. He found it equally hard to believe that this stranger, this Greneknighte, this man whose business card defined him as a *privatier*, was about to behead him, here, somewhere in North Wales, in the middle of the twentieth century – if he did nothing to stop him.

'But he stood there waiting, trying to retain a sense of dignity.

'Greneknighte indicated the rock. "That stone might have been put there for our purpose," he said. "If you wouldn't mind removing your scarf and jacket, it would make my task easier. The nape of the neck needs to be bare. I wouldn't want to slice through the leather collar. That jacket looks nearly new and must have cost a pretty penny."

'Gavin stared at him – the huge figure dressed in green leather, most of his face hidden behind the helmet's visor, the monstrous axe he was holding in his hands. There was something about his manner of speech, the vibrant tone of his words, but Gavin's thoughts whirled and would not settle. Feeling cold and exposed, despite the thick pullover he was wearing, he took off his scarf and jacket and placed them on the stony ground. He hugged his arms and glanced up. The sky was brighter, bluer than before, but there was no sign of the sun.

'"It will be cold down here a while longer," Greneknighte said, glancing at his watch. He looked at Gavin. "Let's complete our business, then you can stop shivering."

'Gavin nodded. He had come so far to face this moment. It would be a betrayal of himself if he refused to bow his head to the other man. But as he was here of his own free will, he knew he could still turn round and walk back the way he had come. He wondered what Greneknighte would do if he told him he had changed his mind.

'He knelt down in front of the block and found its height was indeed ideal for the purpose. He glanced at the ground on either side for signs of old blood that had been spilt here before, but the only thing noticeable was the disturbed earth where Greneknighte had uncovered his half of the gold bar. Stones dug into his knees. He wasn't sure where he should place his arms.

'"Make sure your neck is clear of the stone. I don't want to blunt the blade after spending so long sharpening it."

'The voice came from somewhere above and behind him. Gavin felt a rough hand rub his neck, as though the man were brushing sawdust from a block of wood he was about to split. He trembled at the touch, but his mind was calm. The worst was over, he thought dully. He sensed the body behind him tensing like a giant spring, the axe raised high and the rush of air as it fell, and some impulse of survival caused him to flinch, his neck shrinking from the stroke at the last second, so that the blade passed harmlessly by.

'"Not quite so courageous as you imagined, Sir Gavin. I think you only needed one stroke in that hall filled with well-dressed bankers and their wives a year ago."

'Gavin heard him shift his feet.

'"Now, if you could remember the bargain we made and keep still this time, so my axe can find its mark."

'Gavin found himself thinking of his motorcycle parked not far away, back down the mountainside, beside the track he and Bertilak's son had taken not much more than an hour before, and it was hard to imagine the boy riding the Triumph around his father's estate sometime in the future. He thought of the red petrol tank with its silver pentagram he had drawn: Axe, Gold, Chastity, Motorcycle and Chapel; he had found them all and here was the Axe come round again to haunt him. *Here comes a chopper to chop off your head*, that's what he'd sung as a child. He remembered the Lady slipping into his room each morning in her silver slippers, and the belt she had given him, which he wore beneath his shirt. The stone was cold against his throat, as he heard, for a second time, the swish of air above his bent head – and again, nothing. No blinding moment of pain, no spouting of blood, no severed consciousness. Just Greneknighte chuckling to himself.

"'A blow for a blow, a flinch for a flinch.'"

'But Gavin was suddenly angry. "Stop playing games with me! I haven't come all this way for that. Do what you have to do and let's get it over with!"

"'As you wish, young sir. Make yourself ready.'"

'And as Gavin waited and he heard a long, deeply drawn breath, it sounded as if the man were winding himself up for the blow. He imagined the axe swinging round Greneknighte's head like the sails of a demonic windmill, before it crashed down upon his white neck, stretched out like a goose's on a butcher's bloody chopping block.

'He felt the rush of air beside his ear, a sharp pain like a wasp sting on his neck, and then the ringing blade was swinging away from him again. Overjoyed, Gavin sprang to his feet and turned to face his tormentor. He put his hand to his neck, where warm blood was trickling from the place where the blade had nicked his flesh. Greneknighte was standing a few feet away, the axe held loosely in one hand.

"'That's it!' Gavin shouted. "A blow for a blow. And now I've fulfilled all the terms of our agreement. It's finished, and I can go home."

'Greneknighte nodded. "You have indeed," he said, "and I offer my congratulations. Our New Year's Day game is finished, and you are hereby absolved of your obligations. And I must say, when I stood in your hall and saw you all in your fine clothes, I didn't expect there would be one among you with the courage to come and do what you have done." He paused, looking hard at Gavin, the visor still covering his face, but leaving his mouth free. "However, I fear I have tested you a little more than you know."

'"What do you mean?"'

'Gavin had picked up his scarf and jacket, and was holding the scarf to his neck to stop the bleeding. He felt cold and shaken. He wanted to sit down, but did not think it a good idea with Greneknighte standing there.

'"The first stroke was a feint, causing you no harm. Which was only fair considering the way you scrupulously kept to our other bargain on the first evening, giving me the kiss from my wife you had gained during the day. The second stroke was similar. I left your neck ungrazed as on the second evening, you also gave up your winnings honestly. But the cut to your neck is for the third evening, when you were not as truthful as before, and though you gave up my wife's three kisses and the gold coin, you kept hidden the charmed belt she had given you. But for this, I do not blame you. Your fault didn't lie in a secret desire for my beautiful wife, but in a love of your own life. And for that, I think you can be forgiven."'

There were gasps around me as the twist in Henley's tale sank in. And having forgotten how the original poem ended, I must confess to being similarly caught out. I was relieved, though, by the knowledge that Henley would only require a few more minutes to get Gavin back to London and the story's loose ends tied up. But when I glanced at him, I was surprised to see his body tensed to continue, his face more strained than before; as though he did not believe his narrator's role was over yet, as though there was more to this tale than I realised.

'Greneknighte paused,' Henley resumed, once his audience were quiet again, 'perhaps to observe how these revelations were being received, and then with a certain theatricality, which Gavin recognised well, he removed his helmet and Gavin found himself face-to-face once more with Lord Bertilak. He flushed at the realisation of how he had been tricked by both of them; at the way the Lady had deceived him. A wave of indignation overcame his earlier weakness.

'"But why? What's been the point of all this? Have you any idea what I've been through?" He stared at his host. "And you tell me this has all been a… game?!"

'"Of sorts, yes. But perhaps 'test' would be a more useful word."

'"A test of what?"

'"Your honesty, your truthfulness. We live in an age when truth no longer seems to matter; when politicians and the newspapers have made facts and opinions indistinguishable."

'Around them, Gavin sensed the light was changing. A bird had perched on the tree on top of the mossy mound that was the chapel roof. The sound of plunging water was louder in his ears.

'"My mother-in-law – I'm sure you were introduced during your stay – has certain powers that seem like leftovers from an earlier age, when the world was simpler than it is today. My wife openly calls her a witch. She devised this version of an old game which you and I have played out together."

'"So you rode to London to try it out?"

'"Yes."

'"And why choose us?"

'"Because I knew you were bankers. Men, and women too, I suppose, with an ancient reputation for dishonesty."

"'I see."

'Gavin was growing tired of the discussion and Greneknighte's – or rather Bertilak's – attempts to justify and explain away the improbable. The sense of exhaustion had returned. He felt hungry. He wanted to rest because it really was too much.

"'You look rather done in, which doesn't surprise me. Let me make a suggestion. I can give you a lift on the Norton back to where I expect you left your motorcycle at the start of the track over the mountain. Then, join me for some breakfast. Spend another day here – as long as you like, if you wish to recover. It's entirely up to you." He paused. "And one more thing. I'd like you to take your half of the gold back to London with you. If you wish, you can see it as a kind of reward for your courage and honesty." He bent down and picked up one half of the bar, handing it to Gavin. Then he removed a glove and offered his hand. "I hope there are no hard feelings between us."

'Gavin stared at the large hand that protruded from the green leather sleeve, as though it were a shoot sprung from something growing here in the wilderness. He did not feel inclined to take it, and he wondered what would happen to the other half of the gold bar that was still lying on the ground, but weariness overcame him and he gripped Bertilak's fingers briefly. And as he did so, he recalled how he had been greeted by a similar handshake four days before, in quite different circumstances. But the giant axe remained as a reminder of what had taken place on the mountain. That and the blood that trickled from the cut on his neck, and the half of the gold bar he carried in his hand.

'He followed Bertilak around the mound of earth and rock until they reached his machine, which Gavin recognised from the year before. He gazed about him, looking for a track that had brought his opponent – who now turned out to be his host – here, and saw the cliffs of the gorge stretching up towards the distant sky. Bushes and a few trees clung to the rocky walls; the falling water, not locked in winter's embrace as on the other side of the mountain, splashed nearby; a hawk of some kind cried overhead. No man's hand had touched these stones, no woman's neither; no axe had cut the wood, no spade had dug the earth or directed the water – the place with its hollow mound, its so-called chapel, was as untouched as if it were a part of the original creation. Only the tyre tracks that led through the stream and away down the gorge indicated a human presence, a reminder that this age he lived in was—'

The Anthropocene. The word hummed in my head, so that I wasn't sure whether I had thought it or Henley had spoken it. It was a word so freshly minted, so shiny with newness that it probably existed only in online dictionaries; it identified the geological age in which we lived, a period, no more than a shaving of time, dominated by human influence over climate and the environment. Would Henley be aware of the existence of such a word? I stared at him, for it was not this word alone that was surprising. I wondered if anyone else had noticed his renewed shift of voice, his transition into a mode of language that could only be called poetic. How was he able to do this? Were these phrases he knew by heart? Although he denied it, were they written down somewhere? The length of the story had assumed improbable proportions, but though he was obviously weary, his voice had hardly faltered all evening. It rose and fell above the engine's beat, the seagulls that cried out even in darkness. Despite the night air, the chill that rose from the water that surrounded us, he continued to sit in the stern in his black suit, his face fixed upon us, his listeners, as he opened his mouth to continue.

'Bertilak slipped the axe inside the leather cover that was slung over the handlebars and pulled it over his shoulder. He kick-started the engine and Gavin climbed on, gripping the parcel rack behind him, as he had no wish to hold on to Bertilak. The sound of the engine bounced off the rocks as they splashed through the stream, following the path out of the gorge and over the crest of a hill into the sunlight. And there, on the skyline above them, they saw a stag. It turned its great head of antlers to watch them as they passed, and Bertilak braked.

'"That's him," he said. "He's the one we'll be after next time. He'll have to do more than just look the part then."

'Without waiting for a reply, he opened the throttle and brought them down to where the Triumph waited. Gavin got off and Bertilak turned to him.

'"I expect to see you for breakfast, young fellow."

'And, with a wave of his hand, he rode away towards the house.

'Gavin stood looking at the Bonneville, happy to find it where he had left it, pleased that Bertilak's son would be unable to claim it. A year ago, he had not been interested in riding a motorcycle or the drudgery required to maintain it in a roadworthy condition, but he felt differently now.

The arcane knowledge contained in the workshop manual he had mastered; his newly acquired ability to adjust or repair the gears and brakes, the piston rings, the bearings and sprockets, the tappets, rockers and camshaft pinions – the simple task of lubricating each moving part of the machinery – gave him great satisfaction.

'He placed his half of the gold back in the saddlebag and, as he had grown accustomed to doing, he patted the saddle in greeting and wheeled the machine back onto the track. He put on his silver helmet and felt in his jacket pocket for the key. As his fingers closed on it, he realised there was something else there too; something he had not noticed when the light was still a pearly grey and his mind was feverish with the thought of the task that lay ahead. He pulled out the key and found it was entangled with a gold bracelet that must have been slipped into the pocket earlier. Only the Lady could have put it there, sometime the previous evening, he supposed. He writhed at the feeling of betrayal, of how she had hidden the pyjamas she had given him and then made him get out of bed naked so she could fasten her belt with its magical properties around his waist; and she had made him swear not to tell her husband about the gift, part of his 'winnings' for the day, when all the time, she had been revealing the details of their encounters to him. But she could not have told him about the bracelet, as Bertilak had not mentioned it.

Gavin looked at it more closely and recognised it as the one she had worn on each of the three mornings. Hanging from the delicate chain was the small oval charm on which he now saw the words *Amor vincit omnia* were inscribed.

Love conquers all. But what kind of love, Gavin wondered; spiritual or carnal? He thought of the beheading game he had played out with her husband; the savage place where the Green Chapel lay. What had any of that to do with love? And what was her intention in giving the bracelet to him? Might she still be playing a game that was not yet over? Without her husband's knowledge?

'His mind spinning, as though he were unable to engage the gears that controlled it, Gavin followed Bertilak back down the track. He found it difficult to conceive that he was free to ride away and take the roads that would lead him home. Roads where there were cars and lorries and drivers sitting at the wheels, where life was what one expected it to be. Except that he wasn't free. He was still caught in the Lady's web; her two gifts to him remained in his possession. One her husband knew about, and one he did not.

'He saw Bertilak turn off the track and cross the bridge to the house. He felt his hand tighten on the throttle. He didn't need to collect his belongings, which he had been reluctant to take earlier, as if he wanted an excuse to be able to return. This was the moment, if he wanted it badly enough, when he could turn his wrist, accelerate back out onto the road, and after a year of torment, leave all behind him. He had kept his side of the bargain and behaved honestly – *Well, almost honestly*, a voice reminded him – unlike Bertilak and the Lady, who had deceived him.

'Bertilak had stopped his machine on the gravel and turned to watch him. From round the side of the house, Gavin saw the Lady stepping out of the early-morning shadows and into the light. Her long russet hair gleamed, and he wondered if her green woven belt really had protected him. He would never know, and nor could he bring this chapter of his life to an end if he held on to it. With an abrupt swerve, he steered the Triumph alongside the Norton and dismounted.

'His legs nearly gave way as they took his weight, and he realised how hungry and thirsty he felt, but he would not stay long. He would not accept any more of their ambiguous hospitality. They were looking at him as he tried to compose himself, and he was sure they had exchanged some words. He unzipped his jacket with a shaky hand, as if he intended to take the belt off out here in the cold morning air. And what of the bracelet? Was he going to return that too, in front of her husband?'

Henley paused. This must be the end of the story, I thought, although from what I recalled of the original poem, there was no return to the castle, no further meeting between the brave knight and the Lady. Henley took another puff on the cigar he held in his fingers. I could hear the radio in the wheelhouse and thought our return to the Barrier could not be far off. Henley seemed to be staring at us, his audience, like an actor who has forgotten his lines. But his expression was blank, as though the loss of memory was more serious than that, as if he was no longer even sure of the part he was playing. Apart from the throb of the engines, beating back against the ebbing tide, there was a strange silence and I could sense around me the anxiety that we might be left without a conclusion to the story that had shaped the evening.

'Gavin is about to return the Lady's green belt, Mr Henley. He and Bertilak and the Lady are all standing outside the castle – sorry, the house.'

It was Lovell who came to the old man's assistance. Henley looked at him and I saw his eyes become focused. He nodded and, with a sudden gesture, tossed the stub of the cigar he had been smoking over the side. The wind that blew from somewhere far out over the sea, and brought with it the smells of salt marsh and swirling mud and water, drowned out the hiss of its extinguishing, that I was left to imagine.

'Thank you, my friend,' Henley said quietly.

However, he did not begin again, and the feeling grew in me that he was reluctant to finish what he seemed to have started so long ago. I saw his eyes resting on Lovell's distant cousin. But then he leaned forward and started to speak.

'The confusion and uncertainty in Gavin's mind must have been visible in his face, because Bertilak reached out to touch his arm.

'"There's no rush, young fellow. We have all the time in the world. I fear your start to the New Year has been somewhat stressful. If you don't mind my saying so, I suspect you're not in the best condition for the long journey to London. As I suggested earlier, you'd be better advised to rest up here today and then set out when you're refreshed tomorrow morning."

'Gavin felt his resolve weaken. His fingers still held the zip he had only partly unfastened.

'Lady Bertilak stepped forward. He saw she was still in her morning gown. "By the blood on your shirt, I can see you have a cut that should be looked at. Come into the kitchen so we can attend to it." She looked into his face. "Then you should join us for breakfast. We can eat in the kitchen as I'm sure you don't feel like chatting to the other guests." She smiled at him.

'And of course, what they suggested was sensible and Gavin found himself following them into the kitchen where he had first met Bertilak. The Lady dressed the wound on his neck with solicitude, but then, after seeing he had plenty to eat, she disappeared into the house. He watched her go with a sense of regret.

'He and Bertilak said little as they ate. His strength was returning after the ordeal of the morning, and he found his sense of betrayal had not diminished. He was resolved to leave without any further delay, and it would be easier if the Lady were not around to try and dissuade him, as he was certain she would. He could leave the belt hanging over his chair. He had not decided what to do with the bracelet. But some other questions had come back into his mind. He finished his coffee and looked at Bertilak.

'"The name on your card, Greneknighte. Is it really yours?"

'Bertilak looked surprised. "Of course. Why should I use a false name? Lord Bertilak, Bertie, Mr Greneknighte, we're all the same person. Greneknighte is the old family name."

'Gavin nodded, unconvinced, finding it difficult to believe anything any more. "And you accuse me of being a banker," he went on, "as if that was something dishonourable, yet on your card you are happy to style yourself a *privatier*. A strange, rather archaic term. I know, because I looked it up."'

'So did I,' the man who had read out the definition from his phone earlier called out.

169

'"Isn't a *privatier* a kind of freebooter?" Gavin asked. "Someone who lives off the earnings of others?"

'Bertilak looked at him with the self-assured smile that Gavin had grown tired of. "Not really," he said. "I live off my own earnings, not someone else's. To me, a *privatier* is someone strong and financially able enough to live beyond the rules of others; in the way that nature knows no laws except her own. But before you accuse me of being idle, while you spend all day working, or playing at working in those counting houses of yours, please remember I run the estate that's been built up over generations by my family. And I mean work in the physical world, with cows, sheep, tractors, hedges, walls, tenants, and yes, even motorcycles. I don't spend my time playing with numbers."

'"Yet your family must have employed bankers to invest their profits."

'"Of course. I would never deny that. But I trust they were honourable bankers. Like yourself."

'Gavin remembered the gold that had been left on the mountain. "Are you really going to leave your half of the gold bar by that Green Chapel, where anyone could find it?"

'"Why not? It will sound arrogant to say it, but I don't need the money. I'll be sure to bury it properly, of course. I quite like the idea of giving back something that's been taken from the earth."

'Gavin shook his head. "I'm sorry," he said, "but I find that hard to believe."

'"That's your prerogative." He placed a last piece of toast in his mouth and got to his feet. "And now, if you don't mind, I've got things to do. It seems to me your mind is fixed on departure, which is a shame, but there it is."

'He came round the table and held his hand out once again for Gavin to shake.

'"As they say, it's been a pleasure meeting you. I wish you a safe journey back to that terrible place. And please have the courtesy to say goodbye to my wife."

'He left, and Gavin sat for a few minutes, collecting his thoughts. He realised it was important to get back to the Triumph, but he knew it would be an act of cowardice to leave the Lady's gifts here in the kitchen without saying anything. He took the bracelet from the pocket of his jacket and went in search of her.

'But though he encountered Lukas and one of the maids, no one had any idea where he might find the mistress of the house. In the end, after roaming through the rooms and corridors, he found himself on the way to the tower chamber where he had slept, where she had visited him three mornings in succession, and where, in their battle of wills, she always seemed to have mastered him. Aware of the emotions competing in his heart, he climbed the steps and found the door to the room open. He had only left a few hours before, yet the bed was made, a pair of folded pyjamas lay on the pillow, and the scent of her presence hovered in the air. He glanced in the wardrobe and found freshly laundered clothes on the shelves beside the tweed suit and the choice of ties.

'There was a noise behind him, and he turned to find her coming out of the bathroom. Her long hair was loose, and she smiled, raising her left arm to her breast to rub the wrist with the other hand, as if it needed soothing, or to remind him of something that was no longer there. He realised foolishly that, though he had the gold bracelet she was missing in his pocket, returning her belt would involve taking off his jacket and undoing his shirt. She was looking at him, her eyes fixed on his face, as if she could see each episode of his inner struggle in his features, and her expression seemed to suggest that her own fate might be tied to his. Or at least that's what he felt, as he tried to summon the resolve to tell her what he knew he should say. This was made more difficult, however, because other than the silver necklace with the single pearl couched in the hollow of her throat, she was wearing—'

'Alarm! Alarm!'

A bell started ringing madly and I heard Phelbas shouting from the wheelhouse. Henley stopped speaking and turned, as we all did, to see Phelbas coming down the deck towards us.

'The Barrier's about to close! There's been a warning on the radio: a tidal surge is moving up the estuary from the North Sea. If we don't get through and are trapped on the wrong side, the boat may capsize.'

As I rose to meet him, I could hear shocked voices around me.

'What do you want us to do, Phelbas?'

'Make sure everyone has a life jacket. The crew will give them out. And then stay away from the sides. We'll raise as much steam as possible to build up speed.'

'How far is it to the Barrier?'

'Less than ten minutes. No great distance. They've said they'll keep the middle gate open for us until we're through, but they can't give a guarantee. The problem is, no one seems to know how fast this wave is travelling. It seems to have come from nowhere.'

He turned on his heel, but immediately looked back, his face clouded. 'Some of you might want to pray to whatever gods you people believe in.'

I looked at him, unable to read the melodramatic tone of his voice, and wondered who the god of banking was. Two crew members were distributing life jackets and I saw guests struggling to put them on. To my relief, there was no sign of panic. It was true that some had left their seats and were casting anxious glances either downstream from where the tidal surge would come, or in the other direction, towards the Barrier, whose warning lights had now changed to red. Across the intervening distance, we could hear the wail of sirens and, in ironic commentary, a few premature fireworks lit the sky on either shore, though midnight was still about ten minutes away. Thick clouds covered the moon and stars and the wind gusted around us.

I saw the Directors had also followed the instructions and were waiting with untypical stoicism for whatever might befall us; in their yellow fluorescent jackets, their elevated rank had been reduced to the same status as ours. And Henley? He was no longer seated, but despite the insistence of the crew and the requests of the women, Lovell's cousin in particular, he had refused the offer of a life jacket and remained at his station. In his dark suit, his head turning from time to time to observe what was happening before him, he might have been a gaunt cormorant perched in the stern, surveying the world that was passing.

I was handed my own life jacket and pulled it over my head. It smelled like old plastic always does, and I wondered if it had ever been used. But there was little sense of an emergency. Perhaps the evening's alcohol had numbed everyone's nerves, and as there seemed no imminent sign of danger, I went back to my seat and discovered others were doing the same. It was as though the main concern was not the closing of the Thames Barrier, but that we might not find out what Lady Bertilak was wearing and hear the last few sentences of Henley's tale. A few seats away, I saw the Interrupter glaring at me.

'Well? Are we going to hear the end of this impossible story or not?' he said.

I ignored him. Phelbas was speaking to someone in the wheelhouse behind us, and the warning sirens from the Barrier sounded very close. I searched for the two women and saw that Elyssa had disappeared, presumably to assist Phelbas in some way. Her place had been taken by Lovell, who had put his arm round his distant cousin's shoulders.

A voice cried out to us through a loudspeaker, and as we all turned to see what was happening, we saw searchlights illuminating the one open gate and felt the steamer shudder as the tidal current, flowing downstream, was squeezed into a narrow channel and the boat was buffeted by the choppy water. Alarmed and on our feet again, we watched Phelbas trying to steer the *Astarte* back between the middle piers, red lights flashing on either side, the dark water ominous with the threat of a steel door that might close and crush us. I heard the roar of the engines as they fought with the churning tide, and saw clouds of sparks flying among the smoke pouring from the steamer's funnel. For a moment, Phelbas seemed to lose control as the boat veered towards the right-hand pier and the stern threatened to swing round. Guests clung to the railings, bottles fell and rolled along the deck, and wood from the bow splintered as the *Astarte* scraped against the concrete. But these dangerous moments passed, Phelbas dragged the boat through the gap and the river grew calmer. We heard the power of the engines being reduced to a minimum.

'I have to check the damage!' he shouted to me, as he left the wheelhouse. I nodded and made my way back to the stern, where I watched the gate that had been kept open for us close with a grinding clang. It was a strange moment – the river's ancient access to the sea interrupted by the use of machinery that had been in existence for not much more than thirty years. The boat floated in the lee of the Barrier, and though the sirens had ceased to wail their alarm, the red lights continued to flash and cast their broken reflections. I wondered who was at the wheel now that Phelbas was occupied in the bow. The wind was in my face and that primitive smell of earth and brackish water was in my nostrils. I heard what sounded like the sigh of reeds, the hiss of some primeval, formidable thing rolling towards us.

Henley was standing in the stern. He turned his face to me and I saw how exhausted he looked.

'I'm almost done,' he said.

Thinking this might be the best chance to bring the story to a close, I glanced round and saw the seats had filled again. But at that moment, the wave that had pursued the *Astarte* at its own relentless pace up the river, swept against the Barrier, demanding entrance. Its crest broke over the top of the gates and, for a brief second, seemed to hang above the stern of the boat. I gripped the back of my seat and watched as Henley, his back to the taffrail, raised his eyes to look at the plume of water, curling like a serpent's tail above his head. Then, with a flick of its muscular body, it lashed out and struck him overboard, along with two others who were close by. Lovell's cousin screamed, and I saw her, Elyssa and Lovell clinging on to each other, as the *Astarte* rocked violently and water swirled around our feet. And above the cries and confusion, I could hear Phelbas, at the helm once more, shouting out his orders, while he fought to regain control of the boat.

No further waves beat over the Barrier's gates, and as the water poured back into the river, I ran down the steps onto the lower deck. A dinghy had been launched and a searchlight picked out two figures in their yellow vests who were struggling to return to the boat. I snatched a torch from the crew member nearest me and scanned the waves.

'Where's Henley?' I shouted. 'He wasn't wearing a life jacket!'

But the man, from somewhere in the Levant like all of the crew, stared at me, uncomprehending, as though he had never heard English spoken in his life. I wondered if I should plunge into the water myself; I felt responsible, but common sense, I suppose, held me back. Others, younger men than me, jostled by my side, hauling the two who had been rescued out of the dinghy and calling out Henley's name, while, as the dark water grew calmer, Phelbas circled the spot where we had lost our storyteller and his unfinished story. A peal of thunder rumbled in the distance, somewhere out over the estuary, but if water fell from the sky there, here there was no further deluge. The dinghy cast off from the side again and the skies on both shores were streaked with fire as rockets raced each other heavenwards. Church bells began to ring, and it was New Year.

In our wet evening clothes, we stared at the beams of light that played over the surface of the water, searching for anything that might be Henley, though I was sure all hope of finding him breathing was gone. But a cry roused us, and we saw the dinghy change direction. Hands reached down into the water and drew something long and dark into the boat. Then they were rowing towards us, lashing the dinghy to the side, and passing the body they had recovered into our waiting arms.

We laid Henley on the deck and tried to pump him back to life, but his body resisted all our promptings. There was a gash on one temple where he must have struck the side as he fell, and Thames water trickled from his mouth. I stared at his pale face, the white shirt and the dark tie tight beneath his chin, which nobody had thought to loosen, as if it would be disrespectful. His hands lay by his sides; his eyes stared back at us. None of us knew much about bringing people back to life. We were bankers, after all.

I could hear a woman sobbing, and then she was on her knees beside him, Lovell's distant cousin. She clasped Henley's cold hands, she kissed his cheeks, and finally she laid her head upon his chest. Lovell knelt beside her, placing his arm round her shoulders in an attempt to console her. A circle had formed around the body and I searched for someone to explain their relationship to me. Lovell looked up.

'He was her grandfather,' he said.

I stared at him. 'I didn't know Henley was married.'

'He wasn't.'

Phelbas had pushed through the crowd and was standing beside me. He knelt down next to the other two and, with large, powerful hands, closed each of Henley's eyes. Then he raised the granddaughter and a tearful Elyssa, embraced her and wrapped a blanket around her shoulders. Lovell rose also, while Phelbas stood looking down at the body, as if there were signs there to read which none of us could see. He turned to survey us, and I had the feeling we were like children to him, staring at the crack in the world through which death had entered.

'There's no Navigation,' he said. 'The networks are down because of New Year, or maybe because of the wave. No one answers the radio.' He looked at me. 'We'll bring him to the wharf and then you, Captain, must decide what to do.'

Startled, I watched him turn away, to return shortly afterwards with a member of the crew carrying a polished wooden board.

'From Tyre,' he said. 'Cedar wood.'

They placed the board on a table and lay Henley down on it. It was the height of a door, but not as wide, and though his feet in their shiny black shoes hung over the end, it would do well enough.

Fireworks continued to explode in the sky above each shore, as if down here on the river, nothing whatever had happened. Everyone was looking at me. Yes, this was my responsibility. I tried to call the emergency services on my own phone, while the crew swept water from the decks and cleared up what they could. They brought a pile of towels so people could try to dry themselves off, though the glass roof had protected many from the freak wave's impact. The Directors, seated at the rear, had barely got wet at all. The life jackets were collected, and I felt the engines shudder as Phelbas increased our speed to bring us home as quickly as possible. Guests kept coming up to the body to stand looking at Henley, and at first I thought they were paying their respects, but when I glanced at their faces, I realised that each one wanted to ask him something as well.

And all that long journey back from Silvertown, past Greenwich and the Isle of Dogs, Limehouse Reach, Wapping, St Katharine's Docks and old Billingsgate Fish Market, beneath Tower Bridge and London Bridge, the melancholy sense of an unfinished story hung over the boat, like the shroud of black smoke we trailed behind us. Finally, in the Shard's shadow, Phelbas moored the *Astarte* by Swan Lane Steps, our point of departure. No ambulance or police car was there to meet us as we tied up, because it had proved impossible to contact anyone, as though the entire city was out partying. But I knew there was a church close by to which we could bring the body until it became possible to make the call.

Phelbas instructed his four crew members to carry Henley. The disaster was present in his face and I wondered how much damage the boat had suffered, how much blame he attached to his decision to sail through the Barrier when the amber lights were flashing. For these things, and especially Henley's death, I felt a sense of guilt, as if my organisation of the annual event had helped bring all this to pass.

With muffled voices, we disembarked and waited at the top of the gangplank for the body to be carried back to dry land. Since the breaking of the wave over the *Astarte*'s deck and Henley's drowning before he could complete the story, the sense of speechless shock had not lifted. No one, not even the Directors, had asked me what was going to happen, but all had gathered, many cold and wet, to follow the corpse to its destination.

I watched Phelbas precede the crew as they carried the board with Henley's body resting on it upon their shoulders. I turned and led the way up Swan Lane to Upper Thames Street, where we turned right and passed beneath King William Street, the same road that brought us, each working day, to the Bank that was our place of employment. Even though the Barrier would still be closed, invisible behind the office blocks, the river would not have ceased to flow as we marched slowly along the drab pavement. Glass and concrete crowded in above us, but the four lanes of highway in this desolate, windy canyon were empty of traffic. We were the sole pedestrians in this first hour of the New Year, and the only accompaniment to our footfalls was the sound of fireworks, still bursting overhead in showers of red, green and gold.

I turned down the alley that led to the church and on reaching the door, I looked back. Phelbas was directly behind me, his sea-captain's cap upon his head, his face grim. Behind him were the crew, bearing Henley on their shoulders, and keeping step with them, Lovell and his distant cousin, the granddaughter in her hooded coat, her arm tightly linked with his; and on the other side, eyes full of sadness, Phelbas' wife, Elyssa. And behind these, filling the narrow alley, were the others, first the Directors and then the entire guest list, I presumed, of the Bank's annual New Year's Eve cruise and dinner. They stood there now, faces pale and pinched from the cold, in the streetlights' sullen glow.

Relieved to find the door unlocked, I turned the handle and opened it into darkness that was not complete. Candles burned in front of a shrine to Magnus the Martyr, whose church this was, but apart from some emergency lamps that gleamed along the walls, there was no other source of light. We flowed into the space that was not deep, but wide, and the last person closed the door. Facing us in the dim light was the altar with a row of candlesticks, and to the right, the pulpit. Phelbas and I passed down the aisle to go in search of something that would support the cedar board, and when we returned with a pair of trestles, we found the crew still bearing Henley's weight upon their shoulders, while the rest of our number sat huddled in the rows of pews.

Then I was standing alone at the front of the church with Henley's long body lying in front of me. One arm hung down and water dripped from the sleeve of his black jacket. He had come appropriately dressed for his funeral, even if it wasn't a funeral yet. I saw that Phelbas had joined his wife, the granddaughter and Lovell in the front pew. They and everyone else were looking at me, waiting for whatever I was going to say. And as I gazed at them in the chill gloom of the church, I suspected that what they really wanted was for me to complete Henley's tale for him.

I realised I had no words to offer, beyond asking for a minute's silence in which to think of our departed colleague, which they had been doing anyway. I waited with bowed head, while water continued to drip irregularly from Henley's clothes. In my head I counted to sixty, and then looked up. I told them they should make their way home, that I would organise the formalities. And to my relief, they followed my instructions, though, cold and weary as they were, each filed forward to the space in front of the communion rail to gaze down at Henley one last time, or in some cases, to reach out and touch him. Even the Directors stood in line, and as the most senior passed me on his way out, cashmere overcoat buttoned to the collar, he bent his head towards me.

'A deplorable series of events, but you have done well. I'm sorry, your name escapes me, but you have been noted.'

He waited at the back of the church for those others who had sat at the top table, and then they departed together, leaving me to wonder what significance, if any, being 'noted' implied.

When only the front row remained, I stepped round the board and spoke to Phelbas, telling him I would contact the authorities in the morning and that Henley would have to remain in the church until then. He nodded, his wife pressed my arm without speaking, and then they too left. Only the granddaughter and Lovell remained. Despite the blanket wrapped around her, she was shivering and her lips looked blue. I took her cold hand and offered my condolences, saying that as soon as my phone was working, I would start to deal with the formalities. She thanked me and said she and Charlie would deal with the funeral arrangements. Her grandfather had never married and there were no surviving relatives who should be contacted. Her grandmother had passed away a few years ago.

She paused, her bright, damp eyes looking into my face as though she wished to communicate something to me, but was not sure how to do it. She was calmer now, her arm placed through Lovell's, drawing him close to her.

'Grandad always liked you,' she said, and, if I wanted to, I could come to his house in Streatham one weekend, and she could show me something she felt sure would interest me. Lovell wrote the address on a piece of paper and placed it in my hand. Then, bending to give the old man a final kiss on his pale cheek, she turned, and with Lovell beside her, walked out of the church.

I heard the door latch click behind them, and stood there considering the things that needed to be done. That I needed to do. But everything would have to wait until the morning. I hoped the police, who had been unreachable when we tried to call them, would not want to ask too many questions. I thought of the walk back to Whitechapel, half an hour perhaps, but at least it might bring some warmth back into my legs that were cold from the soaking my trousers had received.

A pew at the back of the church creaked, and I was startled to discover the man I had come to call the Interrupter was still present. He was scowling as he pushed past me to stand beside the body. He lifted Henley's hand and gripped it in his own. Then he bent down until his lips were pressed against the cold ear so I could barely understand him.

'I'm sorry you're dead, Henley, but I never liked you, with your sanctimonious manners and unlikely anecdotes. I have to hand it to you, though – tonight was something special. A masterpiece. A story to which no one will ever know the end. Did you even organise your death to prevent anyone discovering what happened? Whether the woman finally got what she wanted from that fool, Gavin, with his ethical bonds and his chastity belt?'

His voice was growing louder, and I was about to grab hold of him in case he became violent, but he replaced the hand he had been holding upon the dead man's chest and stepped back. I stared at him in amazement.

'It was a story,' I said. 'Only a story.'

He glared at me. 'The wave that came from nowhere, his death by drowning, almost as improbable as that crazy beheading game!' He paused 'He called you the Narrator. What the hell's that supposed to mean?'

I stared at his face, distorted with anger. 'As I said, it's only a story.'

'But a story has to have an ending.'

He might have said more, but another figure, who must have been waiting in the shadows, watchful until the end, stepped forward to grip his arm.

'You again,' he said. 'You never seem to get it, do you? I wouldn't bother coming into work in the morning, unless it's to clear your desk.'

It was the man I called the Bulldog and, looking at him closely, with his thick neck and small eyes, I saw how appropriate the name was. I could not recall ever having seen him at the Bank, but he nodded to me as if we shared the same philosophy of life, and holding the Interrupter by the arm, he escorted him down the aisle and out into the night.

I stared around the church, silent except for the drips of water from Henley's clothes, to check I was the only one left now. I went and stood by the body and made sure his hands were resting securely on his breast. I placed my card between his fingers, in case the church warden discovered him before I had the chance to phone in the morning.

Making my way back to Upper Thames Street, I was about to cross the four lanes of traffic-free road, when a sense of unease filled me, as if I had forgotten to lock my own front door. There was no key to the church, and I became oppressed by the idea that someone might make off with Henley's body before I could return. A tramp might search his pockets for something of value. I looked around me, as an east wind gusted through the ravine of office blocks, but there was no one in sight. Were they all asleep, watching the fireworks further up the river, or was this just the routine desolation of the City streets once the bankers and moneymen had gone home in the evening?

I turned round and walked back to the church. The smell of candle wax and old hymn books hovered in the air. Henley lay there in front of the altar, on the slice of cedar wood from old Phoenicia, his face still and stern like a medieval knight on his tomb. All he needed was a greyhound at his feet, or his lady beside him. Little pools of water had gathered on the stone floor where the Thames continued to leak out of him. Feeling like a grave robber, I reached into his jacket pockets and did what I should have done earlier, removing his wallet, glasses case, a sodden packet of cigars, keys, some coins and two damp business cards.

I placed everything on a pew and, using my mobile as a torch, I examined the cards. They were the ones he had held aloft for dramatic effect during the telling of his tale. One was Gavin's, with the five letters, *AGCMC*, forming the pentagram he had described. The other was not really a card at all, but a brown holly leaf on which Greneknighte's name and his occupation of *privatier* were not so much printed as tattooed, and as I peered at it in the empty church, I could see that the edges of the dead leaf were tinged with the palest green, as if in this midwinter season, when holly thrived, the river's moisture was bringing it back to life.

Fitt the Fifth

But I didn't catch the train south of the river to the house in Streatham where Henley had lived that weekend, or in the weeks that followed. Both the police and the Reverend Manley of St Magnus the Martyr had difficulty understanding the 'deplorable' events of New Year's Eve and my part in them. I found hours of my time taken up with answering questions, especially concerning the reason why Henley had not been wearing a life jacket, and explaining, explaining; explaining things that could perhaps be interpreted, or described, but not explained. However, I saw both Lovell and Henley's granddaughter, whose name I learned was Megan, at the cremation. She looked sad but serene, in a dark skirt and jacket, a small black hat and what looked like the green silk scarf she had been wearing on the night of the drowning, but the mystery of how she came to be Henley's granddaughter covered her like a veil. What I knew of her grandfather and his old-school values seemed to make any kind of extramarital liaison from the distant past unlikely. Lovell, as he had been on New Year's Eve, stood in close attendance.

Phelbas and Elyssa had made the journey from the river, but in their clothes of mourning, away from their element, the water, they looked ill at ease and out of place. I sat next to them during the brief service and, as we stared at the wooden box containing Henley's body before it sank down into the fire below, I wondered about the gods they believed in and their unknowable names. I tried to picture the temples they were worshipped in on the banks of other rivers, where broad steps led supplicants up from the water's edge and priests dressed in shadows tended sacred flames; I tried to imagine what rites these gods demanded for the dead and whether they could be called upon in extremity in this remote corner of the earth. But glancing at their faces, I wondered if Phelbas and Elyssa believed in gods at all. It seemed from the funeral arrangements that Henley had not.

Here in the South London Crematorium, a man of indeterminate faith, who wore a strange grey cap on his head, conducted matters and spoke a few words about the person we were saying goodbye to. But though I strained my ears to listen, his ineffectual, barely audible voice prevented me from learning anything concerning Megan's grandmother. Lovell rose from his seat in the front row and read an extract from Homer about Odysseus' homecoming, which baffled me, until he told us *The Odyssey* had been Henley's favourite book.

After it was over, I told Megan how sorry I was and apologised for not having taken up her invitation. She said it didn't matter, but they were considering selling the house, which she had inherited, in the spring, so I should not put off my visit for long. We were standing by the entrance to the crematorium, trying to avoid being pushed aside by the mourners for the next service.

'You will come soon, won't you?' she said.

I nodded, and was going to arrange a date, but we were interrupted by one of the Directors, the only one I saw present, despite Henley's long years of service. Few colleagues had taken the afternoon off work, and I presumed that for many, the circumstances of that night belonged to an episode in their lives they no longer wished to acknowledge; as though their acclaim for Henley and his narration of the story about Gavin and Greneknighte, coupled with the events that followed, were like the incidents from some drunken escapade whose recollection was painful.

Avoiding anyone else, I walked back to the station with a sense of guilt my only companion, but, despite my best intentions, for reasons too tedious to narrate, it was not until a Sunday afternoon in April that I managed to catch the number 137 bus out to the house. I hated driving through the city's clogged streets, and enjoyed the short journey, perched at the front of the top deck like the schoolboy I once was, hearing overhanging branches scratch against the roof. And all the way, I thought about Henley and the story he had not been able to complete. Like the Interrupter, like the rest of the company who had steamed through the Thames Barrier in the *Astarte* and who had stood in the church in front of the body we had hauled from the river, I would have liked to know what had happened between Gavin and Bertilak's wife at what I presumed was their last meeting. I would have liked to know how his story ended. And I also wondered about the Interrupter's claim that Henley had provoked, even stage-managed, his own death. Was such a possibility any more extraordinary than the gruesome and supernatural events he had narrated, which he claimed throughout were not fiction?

Though Streatham is not a great distance from Whitechapel, I found myself in unfamiliar territory and was

forced to use my dog-eared *A-Z* (Google Maps I distrusted)
to negotiate Leigham Court Road and a series of side streets
until I reached my destination. The house was a squat,
middle-class home, built in the '20s or '30s, and its air of
genteel neglect showed it to be the property of an ageing
owner. No one answered my ring on the bell, but a car was
parked outside, and thinking I could hear voices from the
back, I opened the gate between the garage and the side of
the house and found myself in a passage that led to the back
garden. I glanced through a window into the garage and
made out a lawnmower, some tea chests, and something
covered by a tarpaulin.

Stepping into the sunlight, I saw the two of them,
Henley's granddaughter and Lovell, halfway down the
garden. They were standing looking at an old apple tree. I
walked towards them, past clumps of scarlet-headed tulips,
an ornamental pond where a gang of sparrows were rioting
at the edge of the water, and a stone replica of a medieval
knight who was gradually keeling over. Bees hummed about
their business in the air around me and the sun felt warm
upon my head. They heard my approach and turned to greet
me. Both were dressed for gardening in gloves and boots,
and Megan had her hair tied up in a scarf.

'So you finally made it,' she said. 'I'm glad, as we may
not be able to hang on to the house much longer.'

'Megan would like to live here,' Lovell said, 'but there's
a lot that needs doing. Her grandad rather let things go in
the last few years.'

'It may be too expensive for us to put everything right.
But this garden is so lovely, don't you think?'

I nodded, wondering if they were intending to live here together, wondering what had happened to her parents and her grandmother. But I did not want to intrude. After all, I hardly knew either of them.

A neighbour had suggested the apple tree was dying and needed cutting down, Lovell said, and we gazed into its branches as Megan reached up to point out a scattering of pink flowers, a handful of budding leaves. I said it probably just needed pruning and then it could go on bearing apples for many years to come.

She looked at me with a smile on her face. 'That's just what I felt,' she said. 'I hated the idea of chopping it down.'

We went into the house and she left us to make some tea. I looked around the living room that, in its owner's absence, had already acquired the melancholy feel of a museum; there was a faded Persian carpet, a sideboard that took up most of one wall, bookshelves, a piano. I glanced at the photographs that were arranged on the piano and picked up one of a young Henley seated on a motorcycle on an empty road. At least, I assumed it was Henley. I only seemed to be able to think of him as the elderly, reclusive figure who had been washed overboard moments before completing his story on that terrible night. But in this black-and-white photograph, his face shone in the sunlight; he stared back at the camera full of youthful confidence, while one hand gripped the throttle of the machine, as if he were about to accelerate away towards a distant horizon behind the photographer's back. I replaced the picture, realising how much of a stranger I was in this house. I had barely known the man, talking to him only in chance encounters in a City bar at lunchtime, or during the annual New Year's Eve dinners. I felt like an imposter, examining the relics of his life, and I could not imagine why his granddaughter had wanted me to come.

Lovell and I sat on the sofa and talked about something or other, and then Megan brought in the tea. I remembered how mysterious she had seemed, stepping down the gangplank with Lovell onto Phelbas' boat, her face almost hidden by the hood she had worn that evening. And now she was pouring out tea into china cups in this suburban home. She chatted away, we buttered and ate the scones, and she told me some stories about her grandfather.

'You know,' she said, 'he often spoke of you.'

'I can't understand why,' I answered. 'We really didn't see much of each other.'

'It was the New Year's Eve river cruises, and you asking him each year if he had a story when both of you knew all along that he would have one ready. He would spend weeks, months searching out something suitable, worrying about its length, whether it would keep everyone entertained. In the end I think that was what gave him more pleasure than anything else. Telling those tall tales.' She looked at me. 'And you gave him the reassurance he needed.'

'And despite the rules, you also allowed Megan to stay and hear what became his final story,' Lovell added.

'Yes, you did. Though I visited him regularly – I only live down the road in Lambeth – I always wanted to hear one of his stories, but without him knowing, so he wouldn't recognise me and get embarrassed.'

I recalled her hooded coat.

'Unfortunately, the disguise didn't work for long and…'

Hearing the catch in her voice, I looked away. I didn't know what to say. I had never imagined that Henley had taken things so seriously. For me, asking him each time had been a casual question. If he hadn't volunteered, I would have found someone else, I suppose. But now I thought about it, I realised that for at least ten years no one else had provided the after-dinner entertainment.

She got to her feet. 'Come with me,' she said. 'There's something I need to show you.'

I rose, and with Lovell behind me, I followed her out of the house and through a door into the garage. She switched on a light and Lovell went and opened the doors, as though these were moments they had rehearsed together. There was a smell of old newspapers and cardboard boxes, grass cuttings and oil. As daylight poured through the open doors, I saw an old-fashioned silver crash helmet hanging on the wall, and beneath the tarpaulin I had noticed through the side window, there could only be a motorcycle. The two of them pulled the cover off, and then I helped Lovell wheel it outside. He parked it on its stand and I stared at the machine, realising with a shock that, in a way, I had seen it before. This was the Triumph Bonneville – the Bonnie, as Bertilak had called it – that Gavin had ridden on his journey to find Greneknighte and the Green Chapel. I looked at the scarlet fuel tank and saw the silver pentagram he had drawn with its letters *AGCMC*: Axe, Gold, Chastity, Motorcycle and Chapel, I recalled. The chrome and paintwork needed some polish, but in my head the engine throbbed and, wonderingly, I found myself reaching out to touch the black leather saddle.

'He still went into the garage to check everything was all right, even though he'd given up riding it years ago,' I heard Megan say.

'It's in pretty good shape for a machine that's been around since the early '60s,' Lovell added.

I stared at them. 'But whose is it? How did it get here?'

'It was Grandad's. It never belonged to anyone else.'

Inside the house a telephone started ringing, and I was reminded of the way Phelbas had rung the alarm bell on the *Astarte* that brought Henley's story to a premature end.

'I'll go and answer that, if you don't mind,' Megan said. 'A friend's been trying to get hold of me all morning.' She held out her hand. 'I'll say goodbye now.'

I was too shaken to say much in reply, but I saw the moisture in her eyes as she turned away to go back inside.

On its stand, the Triumph looked like a prop from a play that was no longer performed, and I realised I wanted to hear the sound of the engine, as if only then could I be satisfied it was real.

'Would Megan mind if we started it?'

'I don't think so.'

I remembered the motorcycle I had owned back in my inglorious student days that had carried me to Istanbul and back, and though it had been nothing like the machine in front of us, I was sure the principles of getting it going would be the same. I examined the controls and opened the choke lever; I gave the throttle a few twists and then tried the kick-start. The engine turned, but did not fire, while Lovell stood watching me, a bemused expression on his face. He had already confessed to never having ridden one, but he offered to have a go at starting it, and at the third attempt the engine came to life. I was so pleased I gave him a slap on the back. He smiled.

'Messing about with Dad's machine when he's out.'

I nodded. 'That's just what it feels like.'

Lovell went into the garage and came back with the silver helmet. He dusted it off with his sleeve.

'You'd better wear this. With a bit of luck, it'll fit.'

The idea of taking the Bonneville, Gavin's or Henley's Bonneville, for a ride had not occurred to me, but I realised it was something I wanted to do. The tank was half full and the engine was running smoothly. I looked at the motorcycle, sensing its power. It must have been over thirty years since I had ridden one, and never anything like this. I hoped I would not look a fool, or kill myself.

Though the visor did not come down, I put the helmet on and did up the chin strap. Then, while Lovell held the handlebars, I got on and made myself familiar with the controls. I nodded to him and rolled forwards into the road. I opened the throttle and found the machine was taking me back the way I had come. Cornering unnerved me, as did the knowledge of the power the engine could unleash if asked, but I turned into Leigham Court Road and rode around the Common. Finding myself on an open stretch of road, and growing more confident, I started to accelerate. The road was empty and unrolled itself before me. Without a visor, my eyes watered as the wind blew into my face and through the lightweight jacket I was wearing. But it didn't matter. Beneath me the wheels spun, and the bushes and open spaces of the Common flashed past. A horse appeared out of a clump of trees and began to gallop towards me, its nostrils flaring, its mane and tail flying, as though it were wild and this were some kind of wilderness. I gripped the handlebars and thought of how Gavin would have worn this same helmet on the journey Henley had described, and it seemed in some way as if all three of us were one and the same person.

When I returned to the house after less than ten minutes, I found Lovell digging up some dead plants in the front garden. He put his spade down and we wheeled the Triumph back into the garage and covered it up, and then he walked to the bus stop with me. We waited in silence for a few minutes while, above our heads, the tight buds of an enormous horse chestnut tree burst open in the warm light. I could see the bus in the distance.

'Did Henley want to kill himself?' I asked.

Lovell hesitated. 'You mean because he refused to wear a life jacket, even though the Barrier was closing?'

'Yes.'

'I think that's unlikely, though he had bouts of depression. He said to me recently he felt he'd lived too long, that the world he'd known was dying.' He paused. 'What seemed to keep him going was the few hours' work each week at the Bank and the annual stories on the boat. And Megan, of course.' He looked at me. 'You know he only discovered he had a granddaughter about three years ago.'

The bus arrived, exhaling its exhaust fumes around us, as I tried to add this detail to the others that still puzzled me.

'And why tell that particular story?'

Lovell had thought about this too. 'Perhaps because it was a last challenge, one as great as Gavin's. And maybe it was also a confession. Almost.'

'Almost? Because he never finished it?'

Lovell nodded.

The bus doors opened with a hiss and two teenage girls, joined by a headphone cable to a mobile that one of them carried, got out and tried to step past us. The one with green lipstick rolled her eyes when we didn't move and she was forced to remove the earplug. She was wearing a shabby leather jacket that looked as if it belonged to an older brother, or a boyfriend, and she had dark, spiky hair. She held out the earplug to me. Her fingernails matched her lipstick.

'Nick Cave, *Anthrocene*. What a fucking cool song.'

For a second no one moved, but then the girls laughed and pushed past us and I heard the other one say, 'He looks the sort who'd know what the word means.'

Anthrocene, Anthropocene. Two versions of the same word. Henley's word. Or had it been mine?

'Are you getting on?' the driver asked.

I shook my head.

'Suit yourself.' And he closed the doors and drove off.

Lovell was looking at me.

'But why a confession?' I queried.

'He told me in one of his dark moods, when Megan was not around, that his greatest happiness in life had come from an unforgivable mistake. But he never explained what that mistake was, and I didn't ask. I think he was a very moral man and telling that story was his way of owning up to something he'd felt guilty about all his life.'

'So you believe the story's true?'

Lovell gave me a long stare. 'Don't you? You've even ridden the motorcycle.'

'But the beheading? Greneknighte picking up his severed head and riding out of the banqueting hall?'

'Wasn't that just poetic licence?'

I could see another bus approaching, but there was more I wanted unravelled. If I was the Narrator, as Henley had jokingly claimed, I had failed to understand the main character's motivation; like a magician who cannot explain his own tricks.

'And Megan – is she really your cousin, however distant?'

'Well, only in a manner of speaking,' he said, looking uncomfortable.

I was not sure I understood, though I suspected he meant they had invented the idea in the hope it would help get Megan onto the boat.

'What about her grandmother? Did you ever meet her?'

'She died before I knew Megan.'

The bus halted, no one got off, and I could feel the driver staring at me. There seemed to be no more time.

'Are you getting on or not?'

'I'm getting on,' I said, fumbling for some coins. I shook Lovell's hand and said I'd see him at work. The driver gave me my ticket.

'Wait!'

Lovell and I turned to see Megan hurrying towards us. In her hand she held something white and rectangular.

'I forgot to give you this,' she said, looking me in the face, so I could see how the moments of sadness back at the house had passed. I glanced down at the envelope she had slipped into my hand. 'It's a keepsake, a memento, whatever you want to call it.'

Puzzled, I thanked her and saw she had written my name on the front in a beautiful, flowing script, as though she had learned the art of handwriting in some other time and place.

'It's also non-returnable.'

'Are you getting on or not?' I heard the driver repeat, as he shifted the gears.

'Goodbye,' Megan said to me as she took Lovell's arm and turned to walk back to the house. 'Thank you so much for taking the trouble to visit us.'

And because she was no longer wearing a scarf, I caught the flash of red and gold as she stepped out of the shadow of the horse chestnut tree and the sunlight struck her hair.

I climbed the stairs to the top deck as the bus rolled down Leigham Court Road, back towards the City and the river where Phelbas moored the *Astarte*, the steamer from somewhere that was almost Phoenicia, that was the setting for Henley's last journey and the tale he had told. I opened the envelope his granddaughter had given me and found it contained a single holly leaf, as glossy green as though it had just been plucked from a bush. I stared at it and thought I could make out the words *Greneknighte* and *privatier*, though I wasn't sure. It could only be Greneknighte's 'business card', that had been brown and almost lifeless when I had last seen it in the Church of Magnus Martyr, and which I had left behind because it seemed to be too much a part of Henley and his unfinished story. And now it belonged to me.

I thought of the motorcycle I had ridden that was now back in the garage; I recalled the characters he had brought to life – Gavin and Greneknighte, and Lady Bertilak. I remembered her final encounter with Gavin in his tower chamber, her russet-coloured hair. And I thought of the colour of Megan's hair, gleaming in the sunshine as she had turned away from me at the bus stop.

She was where his story ended.

Acknowledgements

Grateful thanks to artist Leonard Greco for permission to use *The Green Knight* (2015) on the front cover; to Doug Mogano for his photograph of a 1963 Triumph Bonneville on the front flap and painter Al Saralis for the additional artwork and much WhatsApped advice; to Stefan for the photograph of the author; and to Wikipedia for permission to use the definition of *privatier* under Creative Commons.

Thanks also to the people who provided support and critical judgement along the way. Especially Sita, for the many years of encouragement; my other readers, Danny Strike, Richard Stourac and Ingrid for their helpful, thoughtful commentaries; Faye Booth at Matador for her sensitive editing; and the many at Munich Writers for their critiquing skills, Lisa Yarger, Vivienne Arnold, Moushumi Sarma and Rita Banerjee in particular.

And if this reimagining of *Sir Gawain and the Green Knight* has tempted you to go back to the original poem, but the Middle English seems rather daunting, you need look no further than Simon Armitage's recent translation, published by Faber.